THE MYSTERIOUS MR. SPINES

WINGS

GROSSET & DUNLAP

Published by the Penguin Group
Penguin Group (USA) Inc., 375 Hudson Street,
New York, New York 10014, USA
Penguin Group (Canada), 90 Eglinton Avenue East,
Suite 700, Toronto, Ontario M4P 2Y3, Canada
(a division of Pearson Penguin Canada Inc.)
Penguin Books Ltd., 80 Strand, London WC2R 0RL, England
Penguin Group Ireland, 25 St. Stephen's Green, Dublin 2, Ireland
(a division of Penguin Books Ltd.)
Penguin Group (Australia), 250 Camberwell Road,
Camberwell, Victoria 3124, Australia
(a division of Pearson Australia Group Pty. Ltd.)
Penguin Books India Pvt. Ltd., 11 Community Centre,
Panchsheel Park, New Delhi—110 017, India
Penguin Group (NZ), 67 Apollo Drive, Rosedale, North Shore 0632,
New Zealand (a division of Pearson New Zealand Ltd.)
Penguin Books (South Africa) (Pty.) Ltd., 24 Sturdee Avenue,
Rosebank, Johannesburg 2196, South Africa

Penguin Books Ltd., Registered Offices:
80 Strand, London WC2R 0RL, England

Printed in the U.S.A.

Library of Congress Control Number: 2008024415

ISBN 978-0-448-44653-0 10 9 8 7 6 5 4 3 2 1

For Alan Sommerfeld.

Until the Woodbine, my old friend.

✦ ✦ ✦

The author would like to thank Molly Kempf.
A fellow Oregonian and an Editor
of surpassing skill.

As a writer, I love asking what-if questions. "*What if* there were a place that made birthday wishes come true?" was the question I asked that led to *The Misadventures of Benjamin Piff* series of books. "*What if* there were a girl who didn't know she had superpowers?" led to the *Zoom's Academy* series. But for *The Mysterious Mr. Spines* series I had a whopper of a what-if question. "*What if* a boy found out that he was the son of a fallen angel?"

This was the question that laid the foundation for *Wings*, the first book in the *Mr. Spines* series. This book is not intended as an allegory or to challenge matters of personal belief. I'm not a theologian, and wouldn't want anyone to interpret the contents of this book as my view of what I expect the Afterlife to be like. It is simply a *what-if*. And I hope that, in exploring the limitless possibilities of that question, you, dear reader, can enjoy the fantastic journey we're about to embark on together.

Jason Lethcoe
May 1, 2008

TABLE OF CONTENTS

There are seven bridges between
the worlds and five of them are broken.
The sixth one has no rails to hold,
and the seventh one was stolen.

—from *Bridges Between the Worlds*, a children's story

✦ Chapter One ✦
ITCH

Edward Alistair Macleod had an itch that he couldn't scratch. It had started on the eve of his fourteenth birthday and hadn't gone away no matter how hard he'd tried to scratch it. Edward's itch was in that very uncomfortable spot, right in the upper middle of his back where neither his left nor right hand could reach. So, of course, he'd tried everything he could think of to reach it, including a bent coat hanger, a stick, a wooden spoon, and a flyswatter. But nothing he tried seemed to work. The more he tried to scratch the itch, the worse it became.

It was certainly no ordinary itch.

"You're up, Macleod!"

Edward's thoughts were interrupted by the whiny voice of his least favorite teacher, Miss Polanski. Like most of the instructors at the trade school, she wore a dirty pair of overalls that were stained from years of classroom demonstrations. This was highly irregular fashion for a woman in Portland, Oregon, in 1921, but Miss Polanski was absolutely unlike any other woman Edward had ever met. She wore black, wire-rimmed glasses with lenses so cloudy with oil and dirt that it was almost impossible to see through them. Occasionally she would look down her nose at one of her students over the top of the lenses, revealing eyes that were such a pale shade of blue that they looked almost white. Edward wasn't the only student in the class who thought her eyes were creepy, but she seemed to particularly dislike Edward.

With a wooden pointer, Miss Polanski indicated the top part of a huge sewer pipe that extended down through the classroom floor.

"Get down there and show me the proper way to sanitize a sewer system." She held up the end of a long piece of rope. "Fasten this around your waist and I'll pull you up when you're done."

Edward's stomach turned as he caught a whiff of the rotten stench from the exposed pipe. He thought of the hundred feet of cramped, smelly darkness that he would have to endure to get to the bottom, and he shuddered. He gazed helplessly around the classroom, but saw no sympathy in the other students' eyes. They were all just glad that it wasn't one of them that had been called on to do the dirty job.

How can I get out of this? Edward thought frantically. For a moment, the only sound in the room was the quiet dripping from the copper pipes that lined the moldy classroom walls. Edward wished that he'd faked being ill that morning instead of coming to class. He'd watched other students take a turn at sanitizing the sewer pipe and had seen how awful the job was. Some barely made it inside the opening before emptying their stomachs; something that Miss Polanski insisted was "just part of the job."

Until today Edward had somehow avoided being chosen, but now his number was up. At this point he didn't know what else he could do other than to remain frozen in place, pretending that he hadn't heard Miss Polanski call his name, and hope that she'd choose someone else.

The teacher noticed his hesitation and smirked.

"What's wrong with you, Macleod, afraid to get your hands dirty? I know you heard me, so there's no use in pretending otherwise. Get busy!"

"All right, keep your overalls on," Edward muttered under his breath. He ran a hand through his mop of black, tousled hair and scowled. Then he rose from his rickety desk and made his way to the front of the classroom. Edward felt his cheeks go red and he scowled deeply as he tried to ignore the sniggers of his classmates as he ducked to avoid hitting his head on the pipes that lined the ceiling. His gangly height didn't make it easy for him to navigate the cramped classrooms at the school.

He hated his school and everyone in it. Only one year earlier, he and his mother had lived in a nice little house on Portland's upper west side. It was the last time he could remember being truly happy. He'd taken for granted the warm cookies, soft beds, hot baths, good books, and late nights playing board games and drinking lemonade with his mom. Life was so good then. He never thought he would end up in such a miserable place like this.

Edward's school, the Portland Steel Foundry, was a boarding school for students with learning problems. It had been created many years ago as a vocational center for troubled youths who couldn't seem to grasp basic concepts like English and math. By training these youngsters to do society's most unpopular jobs, the officials in charge of the school believed they were helping society and providing a future for otherwise hopeless cases.

The subjects taught at the trade school were unsavory by most people's standards. Edward's daily schedule included classes like Care and Maintenance of Sewer Pipes, Extrication of Mold and Fungus, Bottle Cap Production, and at the end of the day, Infinite Uses for Ball Bearings. And because they worked with machinery all day, most of the students' fingernails were stained a permanent black from grease and dirt. The work was hard, and most of the boys and girls at the Foundry were of the same stock, well known for being thick in the arms as well as "thick" in the head.

Edward wasn't either. He was tall, thin, and very smart. His stay at the Foundry was supposed to have been temporary. After his mother's untimely death, his aunt claimed that she couldn't handle Edward's "attitude problem" and believed that a short stay at the Foundry would do him good.

The "short stay" had turned into a year.

Edward had just tied the end of the rope around his waist when suddenly a loud ringing echoed through the room, signaling the end of class.

"Next time, Macleod." Miss Polanski grunted. She glared at him over the top of her spectacles with her strange, ice-blue eyes. Edward shuddered. Then, as the scraping sound of chairs being scooted back from desks filled the room, she called after the retreating students, "I want three pages on Eugene Belgrand and the Paris sewer system for Wednesday."

Relieved, Edward quickly untied the rope and exited the classroom. He had a study period before his next class, Bottle Cap Production, and was looking forward to escaping to the library, one of the few places he could hide for a while, undisturbed.

Edward navigated the winding corridors, his head and shoulders rising like a ship's mast high above the sea of other students in the crowded hallways. Several kids glanced up at him as he walked, making cracks like, "How's the weather up there, Macleod?" or "Hey, Bean Pole!"

Edward knew that his gangly, six-and-a-half-foot height was unusual for a fourteen-year-old boy, but having people call him cruel names like *Bean Pole* made him feel even more like an outcast. He tried to keep his gaze focused straight ahead and pretend that he was alone and that none of the other students existed.

A second bell rang and the halls slowly emptied as classes began. The muffled sound of heavy machinery droned from behind most of the classroom doors he passed, and he wrinkled his nose as the metallic scent of seared copper filled his nostrils, indicating that a beginners' welding class was underway nearby.

After a few more twists and turns, Edward finally reached the Foundry library. He closed the weathered doors behind him and gazed at the rows of high shelves that spread outward for several hundred feet. Each of the shelves was stocked with repair manuals for almost every kind of machinery imaginable.

Edward breathed a huge sigh of relief. There were no other students in sight. Although it would have been more exciting if the library had been filled with interesting books, at least there was something to read here. Besides, the high ceilings in the library made it one of the few places in the whole school where Edward felt halfway normal.

Edward grabbed one of the manuals, not really caring which one it was, and sat down. Flipping it open, he scanned the interior while distractedly rubbing the itchy spot between his shoulders against the back of the chair. He had just settled in when a rough voice called out from somewhere nearby.

"Hey, Sticks, I've been looking for you."

Edward bristled at the insulting nickname.

He set the book he was reading, *Gripp's Guide to Gear and Valve Repairs*, down on the stained oak table and looked up.

Wonderful. It was the last person in the world he wanted to see. Leaning against a tall, battered bookcase was John Grudgel, nicknamed Grudge by most of his victims at the Portland Steel Foundry. Grudge leered at Edward from under a curtain of greasy red hair. His usual sidekick, Scott Snerl, a thuggish blond boy who never changed his gray mechanic's coveralls, stood behind him. Both of them had their big arms folded across their chests.

Here we go again, Edward thought bitterly.

He glared at the bullies. He thought of barking back an insult, but wisely held his tongue. Undoubtedly it would come out all wrong.

"Sticks, I've got a question for you," Grudge said, his voice dripping with malice. As he drew closer, Edward noticed that he was holding something in his fist.

"Know anything about *these*?"

Edward glanced down at the steel marbles in

Grudge's meaty palm. He fought hard to keep from smirking. Last night at dinner Edward had hidden those same ball bearings in Grudge's shepherd's pie. A few minutes later there had been a loud shout from the bully's table, and word of Grudge's chipped tooth had spread quickly among the students.

"Nuh-no," Edward said, fighting to keep the stutter he hated so much in check. "I h-heard about your tooth though. Yuh-you oughta be muh-m-more careful. I've heard the puh-peas in the shepherd's pie cuh-c-can be really t-tough."

Grudge's freckled face turned an ugly purple color. Glaring up at Edward, he hissed, "I know it was you, Bean Pole."

Earlier in the week both boys had gotten in trouble for fighting when Grudge had shoved Edward into an open septic tank during Sewer Repair class. Edward felt that his clever scheme with the shepherd's pie was justified retaliation. After all, his brains were his only defense against Grudge's formidable brawn.

"So, w-what if it *was* me? What're y-you

going to do about it?" Edward snapped back, trying to sound braver than he felt.

In reply, Grudge poked Edward hard in the chest with a thick forefinger and said, "Maybe I'll send you crying home to Mommy, Macleod."

The bully looked over at Snerl and then added in a simpering voice, "Oh, that's right. He can't go home, can he? Mommy *died*, didn't she Eddie? What was it from, again?"

Grudge pretended to think and then shot Edward an evil grin.

"Oh that's right, she died of *embarrassment* because her widdle Eddie-Weddie never learned how to talk."

Edward flushed deep crimson. Leaping up from the chair he shouted, "Leave my muh-mother out of this, Grudge!"

"Fight! Fight! Fight!" As if on cue, Snerl took up the ritualistic chant. Soon other students poured through the library doors, alerted by the commotion and eager to see the spectacle.

Edward stood with fists clenched, towering above his adversary. He couldn't help but think that his height would have been an advantage if he hadn't been so incredibly thin.

"Show me whatcha got, Skinny." Grudge sneered, gazing up at Edward. The boy was much shorter than Edward, but each of his arms was nearly as thick as Edward's waist. Edward knew that one solid punch from Grudge's ham-sized fists would practically snap him in half. He glared back, determined not to let Grudge see how insecure he really was.

As the two boys circled each other, Edward felt the uncomfortable itch on his back burn with renewed vigor. He hated that stupid itch almost as much as he hated Grudge. What Edward wouldn't give to wipe that sneer off Grudge's face permanently!

Edward's eyes darted to the library bookshelves.

Suddenly, a vivid picture of one of the gigantic shelves smashing down on top of the bully's head filled his mind. *Yeah, that would do it*, he thought grimly. He smiled cruelly at Grudge as they circled each other, picturing him flattened by the heavy shelves. *Just how great would that be?* Happiness bubbled up inside of him at the thought of it. It almost made him feel happy enough to sing.

No more John Grudgel . . .

Suddenly, as if in response to the thought, the itch on his back blazed with intensity. Edward stumbled backward, clawing at the inflamed area. It felt like a million bee stings!

Just then the huge bookshelf behind the bully teetered, rocking back and forth as if strong, invisible hands were pushing it from behind. A few students were distracted from Edward long enough to notice, and they pointed at the strangely behaving shelf. Snerl had barely enough time to shout for Grudge to get out of the way when it fell, smashing into the tile floor with a deafening *KA-BOOOOM*!

"Aah!" Grudge let out a frightened yelp and stumbled away from the wreckage, shaking. Edward stopped trying to reach his itch and stared wide-eyed at the broken shelves and repair manuals strewn across the floor.

Did that really just happen?

A shrill blast sounded directly behind them. Then a disheveled teacher holding a metal whistle dashed into view.

"What's going on here?" Mr. Ignatius,

Edward's Bottle Cap Production teacher, narrowed his blue eyes at Edward and Grudge. Mr. Ignatius's pale eyes reminded Edward a lot of Miss Polanski's, except for the fact that they looked ten times larger when magnified behind his thick glasses.

"Fighting again?" The instructor pushed his heavy glasses up on his nose. "Physical confrontation is strictly forbidden at the Foundry." He glanced down at the destroyed bookshelf. "Not only that, but you've also destroyed valuable school property."

"It was Edward's fault, Mr. Ignatius," Grudge said, feigning innocence. "I was just checking out a repair manual. He started pushing me for no reason, looking for a fight."

Mr. Ignatius shot Edward an appraising glance. "Is this true, Macleod?"

"N-n-nuh-no," Edward said coldly. Knowing that his stutter would only embarrass him further, he decided not to elaborate.

After a long moment, Mr. Ignatius said, "I don't know what happened here, but I'm sending you *both* to see Dr. Warburton immediately. He'll have to sort it out."

Edward blanched. *The principal!*

As the two boys were marched down the empty hall that led to the principal's office, Edward's itch began to burn again. Thinking back to the incident in the library, he suppressed a shudder. If Grudge hadn't gotten out of the way at the last second, the falling shelves could have killed him! It was exactly what Edward had fantasized about, but he didn't really want Grudge to die. He had just wanted Grudge to leave him alone.

Feeling a twinge of guilt, Edward Macleod sat down on one of the hard wooden chairs in Dr. Warburton's office and waited. The itch crawled uncomfortably along his spine, and out of habit he reached under his sweater and tried to scratch it. Distractedly, he thought back to how the itch had burned when he'd wanted the bookshelf to fall on Grudge. It was almost as if the itch had been something alive, something eager to respond to Edward's need for vengeance.

The more he thought about it, the more anxious he felt. What was wrong with him? If he ever tried to explain his itch to anyone, they would think he was crazy. How could it be possible? Yet he knew with increasing certainty that the two things were linked. The bookshelf had fallen in response to his thoughts. He nervously bit at his fingernails, knowing one thing for sure.

It was certainly no ordinary itch.

✦ Chapter Two ✦

SPINES

Nobody noticed the small, unusually shaped figure that slunk along the edge of the Foundry's moldy brick walls.

The gnarled creature was good at hiding, having done it for a very, very long time. He was short as a stump, and the prickly quills that passed for his hair stuck out in all directions from beneath an old stovepipe hat. But in spite of his strange, almost animal appearance, the creature's beady eyes glittered with deep intelligence. They were eyes that had seen too many things over the years.

His tiny feet made no noise as he crossed the sparse courtyard and arrived at his destination: the overgrown shrubs beneath the window of Dr. Warburton's office. This wasn't the first time that the mysterious Mr. Spines had been to the

Foundry. He'd visited many times before to study his favorite subject.

Mr. Spines's leathery tongue darted across his broken, yellow teeth as he struggled to peer into the dirty window. The windowsill was high, and he could barely see into the office. Cursing quietly under his breath, he spotted a rusted spigot and, after placing his foot upon it, raised himself a little higher.

That's better, he thought.

Soon he spotted Edward, who was gnawing worriedly at his dirty fingernails. The thuggish boy that had given Edward so many problems since the day he had arrived at the Foundry sat next to him.

What has Edward done to get in trouble this time? Spines narrowed his eyes with concern. Edward glanced up in the direction of the window. Quick as a flash, Spines ducked away. He couldn't afford to be seen by the boy. Not yet.

After a moment he peeked back up and watched as Edward squirmed uncomfortably, rubbing his shoulders against the back of his chair.

Mr. Spines's eyes lit with understanding. "Ahh!" he whispered quietly. *It's the itch!*

The door banged open and the scowling form of Dr. Warburton entered the office. Spines pricked up his ears as the irritated principal addressed the boys.

"This is the third time this week that I've had reports of conflict between you two. We just can't have this kind of thing here at the Foundry." Warburton puffed out his walrus mustache. "Your lack of manners and flagrant disregard for the rules has left me no other choice. I'm bringing in an outsider, a *specialist*, who I've been assured will teach you both how to behave. His name is Mr. Scruggs and he'll be arriving here any minute now."

What? Mr. Spines's leathery tongue swept his dry lips with nervous agitation. *It can't be! Not "Whiplash" Scruggs!*

Spines knew that name all too well. He couldn't allow Scruggs to get anywhere near Edward. Mr. Spines gulped nervously. Could it be that Scruggs had somehow found out about Edward and what he really was?

The sounds of barking dogs interrupted his thoughts. A high-pitched voice with a deep Kentucky accent cut through the early evening air, shouting, "Olivier, Mulciber, heel! Heel, I say!"

There was no mistaking that voice or those dogs' names.

It was *him*.

With his heart thumping wildly, Spines spotted a shadowy place beneath a nearby juniper. He had to hide, and quick! He looked around frantically for a better hiding spot, but it looked like that was his only option. He held his breath, knowing that he couldn't make even the slightest sound when he jumped.

CREEEAK! The rusted spigot moved beneath his foot. He froze, hardly daring to breathe. The barking of the dogs was growing louder and closer.

Mr. Spines stiffened, his spiny hair standing up in all directions. Quick as a flash, he leaped from the spigot and darted along the Foundry's mossy wall, running as fast as his short legs could carry him. But it was too late, the dogs had his scent. He could hear their paws pounding into the ground behind him.

"OLIVIER! MULCIBER! Come back here!"

The burly form of Whiplash Scruggs arrived at the window where Mr. Spines had just been hiding moments before. He was a bleached mountain of a man, with pale, doughy features that were crammed tightly into a wrinkled white linen suit. Beneath the brim of his wide hat were two too pale-blue eyes carpeted by bushy, caterpillar-like eyebrows.

Huffing and puffing, the big man scanned the area, carefully examining the freshly trodden soil near the juniper bushes. He stroked his black goatee and focused on a muddy spot near the rusted spigot. Kneeling down next to a small, pointed footprint, his plump face split into a wide smile.

Aha!

He stood, brushing the dirt off of the knees of his trousers and stared off in the direction his pets had gone. Their frenzied barking was now reduced in volume but he could still hear them, far beyond the Foundry's moldy walls.

"Eat well, my darlings," he murmured quietly. His dark eyes glittered in the light of the setting sun as he added, "And mind the prickles."

✦ Chapter Three ✦
SCISSORS

The cellar underneath the Foundry was seldom used except to store broken machinery, furniture, and cleaning supplies. Mold grew on the damp walls and the packed dirt floor was slimy with mud. There was only one small window covered with grime, so the only light that filtered into the gloomy darkness came from the cracks in the floorboards above. Edward brushed at the spider webs that clung to his arm and suppressed a shudder as he looked around. He hated spiders.

He wrinkled his nose at the musty smell and glanced over at Grudge. The stocky boy was sitting next to a large barrel of rusted machine parts, glowering. Neither of the boys had exchanged a word since they'd been locked in the room three hours earlier.

Edward reached into his pocket and removed a tattered deck of playing cards. After shaking them loose from the box, he brushed away a smooth, mostly dry area on the dirt floor with the side of his palm. Then, he took a deep breath and began to stack the cards, balancing them on top of each other until a pattern emerged.

One of Edward's few talents was his ability to build elaborate card houses. It was something that had always come naturally to him, and he'd been making them since he was a toddler. His mother had been amazed when he built his first one, a sprawling structure that covered the entire kitchen floor. Ever since then, whenever Edward felt anxious or needed to think, he would build a card house.

Although Grudge was doing his best to ignore Edward, he couldn't help but glance over at the incredible tower that was rising quickly off of the floor. Each card was precariously balanced on the last. But somehow, in spite of how delicate it looked, the engineering was solid.

"How do you do that, Sticks?" Grudge asked, unable to hide his curiosity.

"I don't know," Edward confessed. He rested a jack of diamonds on top of two other cards. "I just do."

Edward was concentrating so deeply on building the house that he didn't notice he hadn't stuttered at all.

He had just placed the final card on the top of the incredible tower when the cellar door suddenly burst open. In spite of its excellent construction, the gust of wind that followed was too much for Edward's building. As the cards scattered across the floor, Edward wasted no time grabbing them and shoving them back in the box. Heavy footsteps creaked down the long flight of stairs, and Edward had barely hidden the deck in his pocket when a loud voice sounded from above him.

"Well, my rebellious little lambs, have we had time to cogitate over the inexcusable behavior we have exhibited this evening?" the high voice drawled with a Kentucky accent.

Mr. Scruggs emerged at the bottom of the stairs, resplendent in his white suit and hat. Edward noticed that he carried a battered-looking doctor's bag. He stroked his ebony goatee and shot Edward and Grudge a calculating stare. When neither of the boys responded to his question, the big man offered them both an indulgent smile.

"Before we get down to the unfortunate business at hand, I suppose that we should start with introductions." He spread his arms wide. "My name is Belvedere Horatio Scruggs, but many of my students prefer to call me Whiplash. After we become acquainted, you might find that it is less a name and more a description of my extraordinary talents."

The bulky teacher glanced over at Grudge, who sneered back at him. If Grudge was scared, he certainly didn't show it. Edward couldn't help but admire Grudge's attitude. He desperately hoped that Scruggs wouldn't notice how nervous he was.

The teacher smirked at Grudge's display of confidence and said, "Why, you must be Mr. John Grudgel."

Edward watched as Scruggs removed a small notebook from the pocket of his gleaming, white waistcoat. "Let me see," he opened the book and flipped through a couple of pages. "Fighting, disrespect for authority, and what's this . . . thievery?" Scruggs's eyes narrowed. "It says here that you've been caught stealing money from the Foundry cafeteria three times this year." He glanced over at Grudge and smiled cruelly. "Oh, I do abhor thievery of all kinds. I find the taking of things that don't belong to one a reprehensible habit."

Scruggs undid the metal clasps on his doctor's bag and reached inside. Edward gaped as the bulky teacher pulled out the longest pair of silver bladed scissors he had ever seen. Scruggs paused to polish the blades with the edge of his white jacket. Then, after restoring them to a mirror-like gleam, he grasped the handles and closed the shears with a pronounced *snip*.

The effect on Edward was instantaneous. Suddenly, an inexplicable feeling of fear swept over him and the itch on his back prickled uncomfortably. There was something he didn't like about those scissors, something that he couldn't put into words.

He glanced up at Whiplash Scruggs. The teacher seemed to have noticed his discomfort. Edward might have been mistaken, but it looked like an expression of triumph had flashed across his face. Feeling anxious, Edward backed away from the teacher and his terrible-looking scissors.

Scruggs snapped the carpet bag shut and continued, saying, "Now then, there are many ways to elicit a change in behavior. Personally, I have discovered a wonderful cure for thieving hands." He casually pointed the tips of the long bladed scissors at Grudge.

A flicker of fear crossed Grudge's face. "Stay away from me," he warned, balling up his fists. "Come any closer and you'll regret it!"

Scruggs threw back his head and laughed. He seemed genuinely amused by Grudge's threat.

"You are a rare one indeed, Mr. Grudgel. I must say, there aren't many students who would have the audacity to respond to me in such an insolent manner. However, I'm afraid you misunderstand my intent." He lowered the hand that held the scissors. "These magnificent shears are not to be wasted on the likes of *you*. I shall reveal my cure for thievery in due course."

Scruggs walked over to Edward and held the scissors in front of his face. He flashed Edward a vicious grin. "No, these particularly fine scissors are for *you*, Edward Macleod."

Then, with a deliberate motion, he grasped the scissors' handles and snapped them shut with two quick snips.

Edward gasped.

He dropped to his knees on the muddy ground as pain flared between his shoulders. It was agony, the worst he'd ever felt, even worse than during the incident at the Foundry library.

Whiplash Scruggs stood over him, regarding Edward with a look of cold dislike as Edward writhed, trying to reach the pain between his shoulder blades. After a moment Scruggs knelt down next to Edward and spoke in a soft voice that only Edward could hear.

"The pain will be unbearable for a little bit longer, Edward Macleod. But very soon you'll understand why that troublesome itch bothers you so."

Scruggs's fat fingers absently caressed the handle of the silver scissors. "And after a quick snip or two, you'll be coming with me to visit someone who has been waiting to meet you for a very long time."

Edward had no idea what Scruggs was talking about. The pain on his back was so great, he felt like screaming. But he fought against the impulse to yell. He didn't want to give in, to let the teacher know how much pain he was in. He gritted his teeth and choked back the tears that clouded his vision.

Whiplash Scruggs turned back to the spot where Grudge was sitting. Grudge was staring wide-eyed at Edward, confused.

"And now for that cure I promised, Mr. Grudgel," Whiplash Scruggs said. Walking back over to his bag, he reached inside and removed a coil of rough leather rope. Then, with a practiced flip of his wrist, the rope uncoiled and the end hit the dirt with a dull *thud*. It was a whip.

"You can't use that. It's against the rules. W-Warburton would never allow it!" Grudge shouted.

Scruggs chuckled, enjoying how terrified the boy sounded. His hand tightened on the handle of the weapon that was his namesake. He gave an experimental snap of his wrist, and the whip traced an *s* in the dirt floor. Feeling satisfied, he glanced up at Grudge and said, "Sometimes the old-fashioned cures work the best, Mr. Grudgel."

A crack of thunder boomed outside. It was followed by the sound of heavy rain spattering in the courtyard. Whiplash Scruggs smiled inwardly. The thunderstorm would muffle the screams that were sure to come. He removed his hat and rested it on top of a wooden barrel before adding, "And I haven't found a better cure for thieving hands." He smiled at Grudge. "Now then, hold them out palms upward, if you please."

✦ Chapter Four ✦

RESCUE

Mr. Spines rushed inside the weather-beaten townhouse and slammed the door shut behind him. Outside, the frustrated barks of Whiplash Scruggs's hounds echoed down the deserted, rain-soaked alleyway. His breath came in ragged gasps as he slumped against a rickety cabinet. He was relieved that the sudden thunderstorm had hidden his scent from Scruggs's vicious dogs.

"What happened to you, Melchior?" a small voice asked. A white ermine with blue eyes emerged from a shadowy area near the fireplace. She glanced at Mr. Spines's dripping clothes and hat and said, "You're soaked!"

"Whiplash Scruggs is at the Foundry! I barely got away from his dogs." Spines gasped. He walked quickly over to the blazing hearth, removed his coat, and hung it on a peg near the fireplace.

Sariel's fur bristled. "Whiplash Scruggs! Does he know about Edward?"

"Appears that way," Spines replied, examining his torn coattails. The dogs' teeth had narrowly missed him.

"How's he feeling?" Sariel asked anxiously.

"Well, the *itch* is getting worse. It won't be long now." Spines paused and glanced around the room. "Where's Artemis?"

"At the bakery," the ermine replied with a shrug.

"What? I told you both to stay put!" Spines exclaimed. As he spoke, the spines that were visible just below his hat bristled in irritation.

"I know, but you know how he is. He said he was starving and he couldn't wait for you to get back. I tried to stop him."

Mr. Spines shook his head and waddled over to a shabby chair by the hearth. It had taken years of careful planning and hiding to get them to this point. Why couldn't everybody just stick to the plan? Despite being five thousand years old, Sariel and Artemis still behaved like children.

Spines drummed his fingers on the arm of

the chair. They would all have to leave very soon. The itch on Edward's back would only grow stronger over the next few hours.

A bump at the rain-spattered window startled him out of his thoughts. Then lightning flashed, revealing a very ugly, winged creature hovering just outside.

Mr. Spines rushed over and threw open the window. With a flutter of green wings, the creature, a flying toad, landed on the floor. He carried a small white bag in his mouth.

"Mm, 'fanks," the creature said in a muffled voice. Then after dropping the bag, he looked up at Mr. Spines with sheepish grin.

"Artemis! What did I tell you about being seen in public?" Spines shouted.

Artemis folded his wings and replied in a whiny voice, "I was careful! Nobody saw me." He glanced down at the soaked bag. "Besides, it was worth it! Look what I got out of the trash behind the bakery."

The winged toad reached his webbed fingers into the bag and produced a slightly smashed cherry tart. "See?" he said, grinning proudly.

Sariel made a disgusted face. "But it was in the *trash*. Honestly, Artemis, have you lost what little dignity you had left? Digging in trash cans is no way for a *Guardian* to act."

"I've still got dignity," Artemis huffed, looking hurt. Then, after taking a huge bite out of the pastry, he added with his mouth full, "You're jusht jealosh 'cause I found it and you didn't."

"Right. Jealous of your trash," Sariel replied sarcastically. "I think the Corruption is getting to you. You're developing a serious *gluttony* issue."

"Yeah? Well you better watch out, Miss 'Look-at-Me, I'm-So-Perfect'!" Artemis mimicked Sariel's haughty expression. "Arrogance is worse than gluttony. If you don't watch out you'll end up just like the Jackal."

"Don't you dare compare me with *him*!" Sariel growled, her blue eyes flashing dangerously. "Take it back, Toadbreath!"

"Make me!"

Sariel leaped at Artemis, her teeth bared in a ferocious snarl.

"Stop it, both of you!" Spines grabbed Sariel

by the scruff of her neck and Artemis by his wings, trying to separate the bickering creatures. "Enough!" he shouted. "You're both acting like a couple of *Groundlings*!"

The two creatures fell silent at the word and looked up at Mr. Spines with guilty expressions. To be called a *Groundling*, a nickname used to describe the servants of their sworn enemy, the Jackal, was a terrible insult.

Spines glared down at them and said, "Edward's itch will probably reach its peak late tonight. We have to get him out of there before Scruggs can do anything."

"Wait, do you mean *Whiplash* Scruggs?" Artemis exclaimed, nearly choking on his mouthful of cherry tart. "How come he's here?"

"Why *else* would he be here? He knows about Edward, stupid." Sariel gave Artemis a withering look.

"Sariel, were you able to repair the Oroborus?" Spines asked, changing the subject. He was eager to hear how repairs to the magical weapon were progressing.

The ermine nodded. "I think so. I was able

to use a small quantity of silver to fill in the corroded parts, and it seemed to help. The Groundling we stole it from didn't care for it very well."

Sariel scampered over to a small box by the hearth and removed a large, rusted-looking ring from inside. She handed it to Spines, who examined it carefully, noting the repair work. The ring was worn and pitted all over its surface, and made from a strange metal that gleamed redly in the firelight. It had a picture of a serpent biting its tail etched into its surface.

Mr. Spines turned it over in his hands a couple of times, and then, holding it out in front of him, said a strange guttural word in a commanding voice.

"Nsh!"

The ring glowed for a moment, forming a fiery circle. Spines gazed at it, carefully noting the repaired areas. After a moment he spoke.

"Well done. The repairs seem to be holding."

Sariel beamed back at him.

Spines stared, transfixed, into the center of the ring. He narrowed his eyes in concentration, gathering his will. Then he hissed another word through his broken, yellow teeth.

"*Qadosssssss . . .*"

The ring's fire turned from red to a bright blue. The icy flames danced around the edges of the ring, casting long shadows in the tiny room.

"It's working!" shouted Artemis, his wings fluttering with delight. "You did it, Sariel!"

The toad had no sooner said this than the flames around the areas that the ermine had repaired began to falter. Moments later, the fire that surrounded the glowing circle began to fade and then flickered out.

Sariel glanced over at Spines's disappointed expression. She grabbed her fluffy tail in her front paws and fiddled with it nervously. Mr. Spines let out a long, disappointed sigh and handed the ring back to her.

"It's going to take twice as much of my power to keep it lit. I'll have to sing a Song of Ignition to keep it going, and that won't be easy."

"It's hard to change what it *is*, sir. Silver is the purest metal I could find, but the Oroborus only wants to work with the Jackal's fire. I can keep trying, though," she said meekly.

Spines paused to scratch his stubbly chin before replying. The Jackal used very dark sorcery to create the magic rings. It made sense that they responded best to his evil power. "Well, it's the best we can do for now. Hopefully it will be enough to get Edward out of the Foundry and onto the train to Los Angeles."

"Los Angeles!" Artemis exclaimed. The fat toad's eyes rolled with fright. "But, sir, the place is crawling with Groundlings. They'll find us for sure!"

Spines nodded and adjusted his small, leather gloves. He knew how dangerous the Jackal's servants were and could understand why Artemis was afraid. However, at this point, it was either stay in Oregon and be found by Whiplash Scruggs or escape to his secret hideout in California.

"We need to stick to the plan. It's the perfect place to hide. The Jackal wouldn't expect Edward to be hidden right where his army is thickest," Spines said, giving the toad a crooked smile. "Besides, if all goes well we won't be there very long. By tomorrow evening we'll be back in the Woodbine."

"But Melchior, what about the contract you signed with the Jackal? You know how he is. If we go back, he'll send his whole army after us!" Artemis croaked. He glanced worriedly around the tiny room, as if expecting the Jackal's evil forces to show up at any second.

Spines waved his hand dismissively. "We've already gone through this. You knew that this day would come eventually." He checked his rusty pocket watch. "We're going to leave at midnight. That should give us enough time to pack." He licked his yellow teeth and glanced at Artemis. The toad stared back at him, his fearful expression made ridiculous by the big globs of cherry tart smeared around his lips.

"And wipe that mess off your face, Artemis. It's going to be shocking enough for Edward when he sees us for the first time as it is."

✦ Chapter Five ✦

CARDS

"My hands. Look at my hands, Sticks!" Grudge moaned, staring at his swollen fingers and palms. Scruggs's terrible whip had scored deep red welts with painful accuracy.

"Hang on, I'll t-tuh-try to find s-something you can w-wrap them up with," Edward said. He pulled against the heavy iron chain that Scruggs had fastened to his leg, gritting his teeth against the burning itch on his back as he stretched out trying to reach an old tarpaulin. The other end of the chain was secured to one of the cellar's cement posts, allowing him a circle of movement of only about five or six feet.

Now that Edward and Grudge had experienced Whiplash Scruggs's disciplinary measures together, they'd forged a kind of truce. All of their prior disagreements seemed petty compared to the situation they were currently in.

Edward stretched his skinny frame as far as he could. *Almost!* His back prickled uncomfortably as his fingers just brushed the edge of the old tarp. He tried again to reach it, the manacle around his foot biting painfully into his flesh as he stretched, pulling as hard as he could. He could see the edge of the tarp just at the end of his fingertips. If he could just grab the edge of it . . .

Got it!

"Hurry up, Sticks. I think they're bleeding!" Grudge complained.

Edward gave the lightweight cover a couple of furious tugs. It came loose in a shower of dust, sending a box of nails that was resting on top of it clattering to the floor.

Edward returned to where Grudge was chained, tearing the moldy tarp into long, thin strips as he went. They weren't the cleanest bandages, but they would have to do.

"Hold out y-your hands," Edward said.

Grudge extended his red palms and Edward tried to wrap them the best he could. It was slow going because every time he wrapped a strip of cloth around Grudge's hands, Grudge would howl with pain and jerk them away. Secretly, Edward was surprised that the bully was acting like such a baby. He knew that his palms hurt, but they could have been much worse. Most of the redness on Grudge's palms was due to welts and not blood.

When he'd finished the bandaging, Grudge sagged back against his cement pillar, looking like a wounded soldier.

"Thanks, Bean Pole."

"N-no problem," Edward replied awkwardly. He hardly noticed the insulting nickname. He glanced down at the manacles on his foot, feeling frustrated. He couldn't figure out why the chains were necessary. The only way out of the cellar was through a small, dirty window set high up on the wall. Unless Scruggs expected them to fly, there seemed to be no possible way to escape.

"How long do you think he'll keep us down here?" Grudge asked.

"Who n-nuh-knows?" Edward replied glumly. "B-before this, I th-thu-thought the worst thing that would have happened to us for f-fighting was a simple detention."

"Hey, what happened when he came after you with those weird scissors of his?" Grudge asked, leaning forward curiously. "The way you acted when he snipped them shut was like you were being tortured or something."

"Yeah, it f-felt like it," stuttered Edward, recalling the encounter a few hours earlier. He had no idea why the scissors had done that to him, either. But he was sure that Scruggs knew exactly what he was doing. By the way he'd talked, it seemed that he knew more about Edward's itch than he himself did.

The painful itch still burned from the encounter, but not as much now that Whiplash Scruggs was gone. Out of habit, Edward reached into his pocket for his playing cards.

As he began building a new house, he felt the familiar calm settle inside of him. He began to model the house after the cellar they were in, hoping that in doing so he could think of a way to escape.

"I'll tell you this much. If my parents ever

found out about this, they would give Warburton an earful," Grudge moaned. "We've got to get out of here, Sticks. I don't want to be here when he comes back."

"I know. I'm working on it," Edward replied, absorbed in his project. The card walls were up, scaled perfectly to their surroundings. He glanced up from the cards to the dirty window high above them. *Now, if there were just some way to get up there.*

He began to build a bridge out of the playing cards, connecting them to the card house cellar walls. As the structure began to take shape, Edward's mind drifted to the inventory in the cellar, picturing each item in acute detail. *Sawhorse, drill bits, a table with a broken leg, two barrels of hex nuts, a gearbox . . .*

He put the cards that would act as trestle supports in place.

A candlestick, three pulleys, six-and-a-half feet of rope, three pairs of mechanic's overalls with holes in the knees, a broom, two hammers, a coat hanger . . .

He examined his bridge. It resembled

a suspension bridge like the kind he'd seen stretching over the Columbia River. Only two cards were left to make it perfect.

I can use the hanger to pick the locks on our chains. Then I can use the sawhorse as new legs for the broken table. Then, if I put barrels on top of the table, could I reach the window? He did some rapid mental calculations. *No! I'm still five feet three inches short.*

Images of the items in the cellar fitting together in different ways flashed through his mind. He saw the exact measurements of each item, estimating precisely how close he was to the window.

Tie the hammer to the end of the rope and use it as a grappling hook. While standing on the barrels on top of the table, I could throw it around the third support beam in the ceiling and then climb up to the window. That should work!

He pictured the items put together in his mind. It all fit.

"I've got it," he said, placing the final two cards on the bridge. He flashed a smile at Grudge, who looked back at him with a puzzled expression.

"Got what?" asked Grudge.

"A way to get out of here. Now, the first thing we need is that coat hanger next to your right foot."

Grudge handed him the wire hanger and Edward began to assemble his makeshift grappling hook. As he worked, he tried not to think of what would happen if they didn't escape. He had the feeling that whatever Scruggs had planned for him with his horrible scissors would be far worse than the sting of his whip.

His itch burned painfully at the thought. *Just a few minutes more,* Edward thought. *And then we'll be away from him and this awful place forever.*

✦ Chapter Six ✦

ESCAPE

Edward's foot almost slipped as he stood on the barrel that he and Grudge had placed on top of the rickety table.

"Make sure that sawhorse doesn't move, will you?" Edward said nervously. He glanced down at the spot where the sawhorse had been positioned to replace the missing table leg.

"I'm trying to hold it steady, but the legs are wobbly," Grudge replied. The big boy was holding tightly to the edge of the table while Edward climbed on top of the barrel. Edward had picked the locks on their chains with an old wire hanger, so they could at least move around the room now.

They'd worked as quickly as possible to implement Edward's escape plan, neither of them knowing when Whiplash Scruggs might return. In spite of his fear and loathing, Edward forced himself to stay on task. He was terrified at the thought of Scruggs finding them halfway through with the construction of an escape route. He was sure that the teacher could do more with that whip of his than just the welts he'd made on Grudge's palms.

Edward balanced on the barrel and uncoiled the rope in his right hand. It was tied to the handle of a claw hammer, creating a makeshift grappling hook.

He eyed the heavy beam that extended across the ceiling. His eyes fell on a small hollow spot near the window. It would have to be a perfect throw.

He swung the rope, letting the hammer move back and forth like the pendulum of a clock. This was going to be tricky.

Feeling its weight, he let the swinging rope gain momentum. Then, with as much strength as he could manage, he let the hammer swing upward in a wide arc toward the ledge.

KA-THUNK! The hammer crashed uselessly against the high beam. The impact was loud and both boys couldn't help glancing nervously to the stairs that led to the cellar door. Hopefully, no one had heard that!

Edward shuddered. This was going to be harder than he thought. Suddenly, the sound of heavy footsteps echoed on the floorboards above. Both boys glanced at each other with frightened expressions.

"It's him!" Grudge whispered. "Hurry!"

Edward quickly gathered the hammer and rope for another throw. He knew that he would have time for only one more attempt before Scruggs burst into the room. He had to make this one count.

Come on! he thought desperately as he rocked the rope back and forth, preparing to throw. *I have to make this.* He grit his teeth and focused on the spot near the window. The unmistakable sound of Scruggs's heavy boots grew closer, causing dust to rain down through the cracks in the floorboards above them.

Edward tried to reach deep down inside of himself, searching for what he had felt when he'd wanted the bookshelf to fall on Grudge.

He needed the hammer to lodge itself perfectly above the beam. He wanted it to happen more than anything else he could think of.

He didn't realize he was doing it at first, but his lips started moving, whispering an unfamiliar phrase. His eyes remained fixed on the spot near the window as he said softly:

Azru Li . . . Azru Li . . . Azru Li . . .

Somehow he knew before he'd even thrown it that the hammer would lodge itself in exactly the right place. It sailed upward in a perfect arc, the claw end embedding itself in the heavy wooden beam with a satisfying *CHUNK*! But as it did, warmth grew between Edward's shoulder blades, hinting that the itch on his back was about flare with new intensity.

"Help me onto the table!" shouted Grudge. Edward had barely time to extend his hand before the cellar door behind them creaked open. Whiplash Scruggs's voice bellowed down the stairs, "What are you boys up to?"

"N-now!" Edward shouted at Grudge who had clambered onto the barrel and had grabbed the rope. In seconds, the well-muscled boy climbed the rope and reached the window. Edward glanced fearfully at the cellar stairs. Whiplash Scruggs's heavy, booted feet pounded down the stairs. Nothing mattered more at that moment than to get away from him. Edward's hands shook with anticipation, waiting for Grudge to throw him the rope.

"Hurry up, w-will you?" he shouted.

CRASH! Grudge smashed the windowpane with his elbow and scrambled through, heedless of the broken glass. He released the rope, letting it swing back to Edward.

"What?" Scruggs bellowed, striding into the center of the room. "Oh no you don't!"

Edward caught the rope and started to climb, but he wasn't as agile as Grudge. His skinny arms shook as he edged himself up the rope, fear and adrenaline propelling him upward.

I'll never make it! Edward could see the edge of the windowpane just out of reach. Waves of insecurity poured over him as he struggled upward. The itch suddenly grew unbearable. He gritted his teeth, trying to push on, but he knew it was hopeless for him to even try. He was destined to fail. He was just a tall, skinny freak that could barely talk. He was bad at almost everything he'd ever tried to do. His mother was the only one that had ever loved him. His father was nowhere to be found. Then the worst of his fears, the one that bothered him the most, screamed a truth he didn't want to hear. The reason his father had left was because he was ashamed of him. He didn't want such a skinny stutterer for a son.

He strained at the rope, his body unmoving. He felt his fingers start to slip.

Please. No.

Suddenly, the vise-like hands of Whiplash Scruggs clamped down on his ankle. The rope rocked back and forth as he glanced down.

"You're . . . not . . . going . . . anywhere . . . Macleod!" the burly teacher grunted as he pulled on Edward's legs, yanking Edward down with his formidable size and strength.

"Let go!" Edward shouted, feeling his grip on the rope slipping.

For the briefest moment Edward saw John Grudgel climbing through the window before he fell. Then he felt himself spiraling downward and was dimly aware of a loud *CRACK* as he smashed into the table. The last thing he heard was Whiplash Scruggs's mocking laugh as the world around him faded.

Chapter Seven
DARKNESS

When Edward woke he couldn't tell if his eyes were open or shut. It was late and all of the lights in the Foundry were out, including any light that would have trickled through the floorboard cracks above. He moaned and turned over on his side in the darkness, pain coursing through his body. His cheek was pressed to the muddy floor and his head throbbed. But it was the itch, not the painful bump on his head that had woken him. It was burning with an intensity completely unlike anything he had ever felt before, like a hundred sharp knives were being plunged into his back.

What had he ever done to deserve this?

He moaned and rolled onto his stomach. His eyes were tightly shut and his teeth clenched. Every muscle in his body protested against the blistering pain. But there was absolutely nothing he could do to make it stop.

Rage burned deep within him. It wasn't fair that he was here. If his mom hadn't died, none of this ever would have happened. He would be safe and happy at home. No Whiplash Scruggs. No Foundry. No painful itch. He'd never done anything to deserve any of it. It wasn't fair! Angry tears blurred his vision as he writhed on the muddy floor.

Life was cruel. Here he was, alone and in pain, and nobody cared.

Why did it feel as though he was being punished just for being alive? Why him? Out of everyone on Earth, why him?

He gasped, his thoughts forgotten. The pain in his back was so intense, it took his breath away. It was so bad that it felt for the first time as though he wouldn't be able to physically stand it anymore.

Maybe I'm going to die, he thought. In the midst of so much pain, it didn't sound like such a bad idea. What did he have to live for, anyway? At least if he died and there was an Afterlife, there might be a chance he would be with his mother again.

Then, just when Edward thought he might pass out from the pain, it changed. It was just as horrible, but instead of an itch, it felt as if there was something trying to rip through his back. Edward couldn't see it, but between his shoulders two black points were slowly emerging. They looked like the tips of large needles that were trying to shove their way out through the skin between his shoulder blades.

Edward screamed.

There was a horrible ripping sound and the two points burst through his skin. The needle-like tips were attached to two big, black objects that flopped out behind his back as they emerged, tearing the back of his sweater to shreds.

What had happened to Edward was impossible by all biological standards, and yet the new additions to his body were undeniably real. From where he lay on his stomach, shaking uncontrollably from pain and shock, Edward couldn't see them, but he could *feel* them. And the feel of them, the pure strangeness of the way his new appendages reacted to the outside air, filled his quaking body with horror. This had to be a dream.

He cautiously reached a hand to his back and shuddered. There was definitely something there that hadn't been there before. He carefully gripped a cluster of the damp things in his shaking hand and gently pulled them around so that he could see what they were.

Feathers?

Then he suddenly realized the impossible truth. What had grown out of the spot between his shoulders were two, slightly damp, ebony *wings*. And they were definitely real.

The door to the cellar above him suddenly burst open, sending a ray of golden light spilling down the stairs and into the darkness. A tiny figure was silhouetted in the doorway. The figure spoke in a strange, high-pitched voice, calling out, "I found him! He's down here!"

But Edward couldn't see who was speaking. Waves of exhaustion and shock were overwhelming him, sending him hurtling back down toward unconsciousness. As the world folded shut around him for the second time that day, a strangely comforting thought occurred to him.

The itch is finally gone.

✦ Chapter Eight ✦

FOUND

As Edward's eyes closed, Whiplash Scruggs's eyes snapped open. Although everyone else in the Foundry was sleeping, the burly teacher had been dozing fitfully, listening for the sound of Edward's scream. It was the signal he'd been waiting for. After quickly making sure that his long-handled scissors were in his doctor's bag, he rose fully clothed from his bed and grabbed his hat.

It was time.

Standing watch by the cellar door, Sariel heard Scruggs's heavy footfalls in the hallway upstairs. She knew that they had only a minute or two before he arrived downstairs. Her eyes grew wide and she shouted into the darkness below,

"He's coming! Quick, Melchior, we have to go!"

Mr. Spines was kneeling next to Edward on the muddy cellar floor. He couldn't tear his eyes away from the new wings that had sprouted from Edward's back. A rare look of tenderness flashed across his craggy face. It had happened! Finally, after all these years, the boy had grown wings.

There was still hope yet.

Shaking himself out of his reverie, he grasped the rusted Oroborus and held it upward, muttering the guttural word of activation.

"Nsh!"

The ring burst into fire, casting dancing shadows on the cellar walls.

Mr. Spines grasped the edges of the ring and pulled. He had to be careful, if he exerted too much stress the Oroborus would break. He muttered a series of deeply magical words under his breath, commanding the ring to obey his will. Slowly, it began to stretch until it was about three feet in diameter.

Not enough! Beads of sweat burst on Mr. Spines's forehead as he pulled, feeling the quivering resistance in the metal as he did so.

Artemis watched Mr. Spines's progress with wide, fear-stricken eyes. His ugly green wings fluttered in agitation as he saw the Oroborus growing slowly wider, inch by struggling inch. He glanced up at the ceiling, and whispered, "Please hurry, Melchior, please! I don't want to be eaten by Whiplash's dogs!"

"Almost . . . there!" Spines grunted.

Suddenly, the flames that burned on the outside of the ring sputtered.

No! Without wasting a second, Spines immediately sang the Song of Ignition that would keep them lit. As the lilting melody filled the air, the flames brightened and began to flicker again.

Mr. Spines ended the song abruptly, breathing heavily. A look of relief flashed over his pale, sweaty features. *That was close!*

Fortunately, the song wasn't terribly difficult, but it still cost him a considerable amount of his strength. His arms quivered as he continued to pull the edges of the ring, coaxing it wider.

Sariel gazed down into the cellar, nervously wringing her paws as she watched Mr. Spines work. He needed to hurry!

Suddenly a deep voice sounded directly behind her. She squealed as a meaty hand closed painfully on the scruff of her neck and hoisted her skyward.

"And to what do I owe the honor of this visit?" Whiplash Scruggs hissed at her.

Sariel reacted immediately, biting down on his wrist with her needle-sharp teeth. He let out a string of curses and dropped her to the floor. She quickly darted down the stairs like a furry bolt of lightning, calling out, "He's found us!"

The ring was now five feet in diameter, wide enough for the four of them to fit inside.

"Grab the boy!" Spines shouted.

Scruggs's Kentucky-accented voice called down from the cellar stairs above.

"Melchior!"

The mysterious Mr. Spines wheeled around at the sound, facing Scruggs with the glowing ring clenched in his small, gloved hand. The two of them stared at each other for a moment, a thousand years of unspoken hatred passing between them in an instant. Scruggs's eyes flicked over to the flaming blue ring Spines held and widened in surprise.

Spines flashed a triumphant, crooked smile at his adversary and hissed the word that activated the magic portal inside the Oroborus.

"*QADOSSSS!*"

The room exploded with light. Shelves mounted to the cellar walls crashed to the floor, scattering bins of nails and bolts everywhere. Dust rained down from the ceiling, filling the dimly lit room with a dirty fog.

But none of the dirt and debris touched Whiplash Scruggs's gleaming white suit. The big man stood rooted in place. His calculating, pale-blue eyes gazed at the spot where Edward, Artemis, Sariel, and the mysterious Mr. Spines had been moments before.

All that remained was a single ebony feather.

After a long moment he spoke, his face breaking into a pointy-toothed grin.

"Touché," he said quietly.

✦ Chapter Nine ✦

RAILROAD

Edward was jolted awake by the sound of a train car's clicking wheels. His face was pressed against something cold and smooth. It felt good on his aching head. He slowly opened his eyes, afraid of what he might find.

They were still there. He moved slightly and could feel the wings behind him, pressed into the back of his seat.

It hadn't been a dream.

His heart pounded as he gazed out the window his cheek had been resting against. He had left a round imprint on the fogged glass. He felt completely disoriented. How did he get onto a train?

He blinked slowly and scanned the lavish accommodations that surrounded him. Crushed velvet covered every wall. Silken curtains with golden tassels hung at each window. The wooden trim that surrounded the compartment was carved with a curling grapevine patterns that looked so real, Edward was almost tempted to reach out and take one of the grapes. Glancing down, he realized that a beautiful table covered with fine linen and a silver teapot was in front of him. He'd never been on a train before; he never knew that they were this fancy.

Then his eyes fell on the passenger that sat opposite him.

"Sleep well?" asked the horrible, prickly creature.

Edward screamed.

"Shush! You'll alert the conductor!" The creature hissed. He waved a tiny finger in front of his stubbly lips. "I'll explain everything I can to you, but you've got to control yourself!"

Edward automatically clamped his mouth shut, not knowing exactly why. If anything, he should be running for his life. But there was something in the creature's urgency that made him stop. He stared at it with wide, disbelieving eyes.

"That's better," the creature whispered, giving

Edward a horrible, yellow-toothed smile. "Now then, you must be famished. How about some tea?"

Edward nodded and then winced as the shaking jarred his already bruised head. The creature poured the tea and Edward's mouth moved, trying uselessly to find something to say. Finally, after a full minute, he found his voice and managed to stutter, "H-h-who are yuh-uyuh-you?"

The creature chuckled. After studying Edward for a moment he said, "My name is Melchior. But you may call me Mr. Spines if you prefer."

Edward nodded, glancing at the long prickles that protruded from beneath the creature's stovepipe hat.

"I-I-I'm . . ." he began.

But Mr. Spines interrupted, "You're Edward, of course. Yes, yes my boy I know who you are. It's no accident that you're here."

"W-well why am I h-h-here?" Edward asked, feeling defensive. "Did Scr-Scruh-Scruggs have something to do with th-this? Am I kicked out of the Fuh-fuh-fuh-fuh . . ."

". . . the Foundry?" Spines interrupted, finishing his sentence for him. "No, my dear boy, of course not. You have been *removed* from that terrible place but you were not 'kicked out.'" Mr. Spines took a sip of tea. "Under the circumstances I would think you'd be grateful. I can only imagine what your thickheaded friends at that school would think if they could see what's happened to you."

Edward reached his hand to his back and felt the tips of the black feathers and shivered.

"You won't be able to use those yet, of course." Spines indicated Edward's wings with a nod. "You'll need a lot of training before you'll be ready to fly." Mr. Spines set his teacup down and offered Edward a piece of shortbread. Edward mechanically took it and raised it to his mouth, too stunned to speak.

Did he just say that I'll be able to fly?

Mr. Spines seemed to read his thoughts and said, "And why else would you have wings, my boy? Not much use otherwise."

"But wh-why w-w-would I want to? F-f-fly, I mean," Edward asked after taking a gulp of tea.

Suddenly an irritated voice broke out from beneath the table, saying, "Why would you *want* . . . you've got to be kidding!"

Edward jumped as a white ermine darted up onto Mr. Spines's shoulder and perched there, shooting him a reproving look.

"All Guardians *fly*, Edward. Only a Groundling wouldn't want to do it." Her blue eyes flashed angrily. "If I had even half a chance to get my wings back, I'd . . ."

". . . be as rotten a flier as you used to be," a croaky voice finished. Artemis hopped out from beneath the table and fluttered awkwardly into the seat next to Edward. "She hates that she lost 'em," he leaned toward Edward and whispered confidentially. "They were the first thing to go when the Corruption set in. They're still there, of course, but they've shrunk down to nothing more than a couple of nubs in the middle of her back." Artemis grinned slyly. "Totally useless. She doesn't want anyone to know. She's too embarrassed."

Sariel, who had overheard the comment, snapped back. "Well it's a whole lot better than having Whiplash Scruggs cut 'em off with his scissors, I'll tell you that much!"

"Tickets please," a booming voice from the compartment next to theirs called out.

"Enough, you two!" Spines hissed, giving them each a reproving look. "Quiet down. We're in a public place."

Edward's blood froze as he was reminded of Whiplash Scruggs and his long-bladed scissors. *So that's what they were for. He wanted to cut off my wings!* The thought of it made him feel nauseated. Even though the wings were brand-new, he couldn't imagine them being cut off. It would be like someone cutting off his arm or leg!

He fidgeted uncomfortably in his leather seat. A new question formed in his head: *How did Whiplash Scruggs know that I was going to grow them in the first place? He showed up with his scissors before, as though he knew what was about to happen to me.*

A conductor with rosy cheeks interrupted his thoughts as he opened their compartment door. As the big man glanced over at Mr. Spines and the other strange creatures, a look of surprise crossed his face.

Mr. Spines waved his hand through the air in a wiping motion and sang a few strange-sounding words.

"*Zeh Lo Meshane.*"

Edward watched as the expression on the man's face relaxed. His eyes looked glazed and out of focus. "Must have been seeing something else," he mumbled. Then he turned to Mr. Spines and asked in very pleasant voice, "Tickets please, Ma'am."

Mr. Spines handed him four tickets, which he scanned and then proceeded to punch. He smiled stupidly back at them and tipped his hat as he left the compartment, saying, "Thank you very much, Mrs. Neusbaum. You and the kids have a pleasant ride now."

Edward was amazed. "How did you do that?" he asked, hardly noticing the absence of his stutter.

"It's an old Guardian cloaking song," Melchoir said with a modest shrug. "I simply changed what he thought he was seeing, telling him that what he saw 'didn't matter.' What he saw was an old woman with her grandchildren taking a train ride to the city, nothing unusual." Spines chuckled. "Humans really don't want to see anything they can't understand. It only disturbs them."

"What d-do you mean h-humans?" Edward asked. "Y-you're a human aren't y-you?"

Mr. Spines ignored Edward's question, slurped the last of his tea and set down his cup with a loud *clink*. "Time for questions later. First we must get safely to Los Angeles. Then we'll be able to talk without the danger of being overheard."

"But I d-don't understand," Edward said, feeling more afraid and puzzled than ever. Who was this strange creature and where was he taking him? "W-why are we guh-going to Los Angeles? I duh-duh-don't even know you."

Spines glanced out the compartment window to make sure that nobody was standing outside. Then he leaned forward with a conspiratorial whisper.

"Edward, the *Jackal* has forces everywhere looking for you. Whiplash Scruggs is one of his best officers and he already found you once. He's probably trying to track you down right now." He saw the confusion and fear written on Edward's face and went on.

"Let me explain. You have sprouted wings because you are not human. The world you're from is called by many names, but the one most commonly used by Guardians is the Woodbine. It's where people go when they die."

Edward's mouth hung open in disbelief. Spines ignored this and continued, "Guardians are the winged protectors of that world. Groundlings are Guardians who 'fell' from the Woodbine and serve their evil master, the Jackal, down here. The Jackal was once a Guardian, but he became obsessed with power and was forced out of the 'Higher Places.' He took a third of the Guardians with him when he fell. While the Guardians' purpose is to protect what is good, the Jackal's only purpose is to corrupt and destroy. Don't tell me that your mother never taught you the rhyme?"

Edward shook his head "no," feeling too stunned to speak.

"I'm surprised," said Mr. Spines, looking

concerned. Edward watched as he cleared his throat and rolled his eyes heavenward for a moment, as if recollecting something. Then he began to speak, chanting the words as if it were a song without a melody:

There are seven bridges between the worlds
and five of them are broken.
The sixth one has no rails to hold
and the seventh one was stolen.
Captive then, the wand'ring dead,
for an epoch the world's turn.
When halfway from the mortal realm,
a builder will return.
His twisted tongue will utter song,
the champion will arise,
But fallen Groundling or gentle Guard,
his choices will decide.

As Mr. Spines finished reciting the poem, Edward's mind raced. The poem didn't make much sense, but there was something familiar in it that he couldn't quite place. It was at the edge of his thoughts, the same way the song had been back in the cellar. What was going on? Had he gone crazy? Was all of this, Mr. Spines, the talking weasel, and the flying toad, a hallucination?

Edward's mind was spinning. If not for the fact that he could feel the wings on his back pressing into the seat cushion behind him, he would have thought it all some kind of strange nightmare. It made him feel both exhilarated and terrified.

"You should rest," Mr. Spines said, leaning back in his seat. He could tell the boy was nervous. Had he told Edward too much too soon? He couldn't risk frightening the boy out of his wits, but he had to gain Edward's trust quickly so that they could accomplish the task ahead.

Edward didn't reply to Mr. Spines's comment. Instead, he leaned back and stared out of the train-car window. He didn't want those things with him to see how afraid he was. They weren't coming after him with scissors, but they were still pretty creepy. How could he trust them when he couldn't shake the feeling that he was being kidnapped?

Edward glanced covertly at Sariel and Artemis, who were fighting underneath the table for the last of the shortbread. If what Mr. Spines had said was true, then they were fallen "Guardians." But didn't that mean that they were evil?

The only thing Edward knew for sure was that he wanted to be as far away from Whiplash Scruggs as possible. Spines had talked as if Scruggs were an enemy, but how could Edward be sure which side anyone was really on?

Edward turned back to the window with his heart thumping wildly. He had no idea who he could trust. He shivered. He had a pair of wings on his back and was traveling to Los Angeles with a perfect stranger who was telling him that he was from the Afterlife. It was too much to believe!

He didn't know what was going on, but he couldn't afford to take any more chances. He had to get away from these freaks and figure out what to do next. He didn't like Mr. Spines. In spite of all Spines had said about wanting to help, Edward still didn't trust him.

Edward leaned back in his seat and pretended

to go to sleep, ignoring Mr. Spines who was watching his every move. Edward knew what he was going to do. He would have to catch Spines off guard. Then he would try to escape!

He closed his eyes.

Shifting to as comfortable a position as he could manage, he pulled his big, ebony wings around his shoulders like a protective blanket. Even though the wings were a comfort, he wished he had something more than feathers to shield him from Mr. Spines's intense gaze.

✦ Chapter Ten ✦

CONVERSATION

Whiplash Scruggs fiddled nervously with his broad-brimmed hat. The situation with the boy had not gone well at all. He walked across his tiny room and gazed out the dirty window. Below him, several Foundry students were gathered in a muddy field, shoveling fertilizer into a ragged-looking garden. He gritted his teeth in frustration. He'd come too far to give up now. He didn't want to think about his Master's reaction if the Jackal learned he had failed to capture the boy. The last time he'd failed the Jackal in a mission, Scruggs had paid severe consequences. How long he'd suffered in the brimstone mines beneath his Master's fortress. The mines were filled with stinking rocks that blistered his palms despite the thick gloves he'd worn. Ages had come and gone as he moved the steaming rocks from pile to pile.

He glanced at his palms, eyeing the heavy callous that each of them still bore.

Scruggs hadn't anticipated Melchior's resurfacing. The Jackal had been searching for the wretched creature for years and found nothing. Why now?

Scruggs scowled. It should have been an easy task. He had easily convinced the boy's aunt to enroll him at the Foundry after his mother died, and then he had filled the school with low-level Groundlings, posing as teachers and waited for the signs. Warburton had been providing him with consistent updates on the boy and his progress. All that was left was to wait for the wings and then *snip*! Piece of cake. The fact that Melchior would dare to interfere was unthinkable.

Scruggs grimaced. He and Melchior shared a long and hateful past. They had been friendly competitors long ago when they were Guardians in the Woodbine. They shared reputations as excellent craftsmen, and their engineering skills were used to develop new and innovative musical instruments for the Guardian choirs. But Melchior had gained the Jackal's favor, after giving the Master what he needed when he needed it most. Melchior had helped design a new body for the Jackal when it had been ravaged by the destruction of the Seven Bridges. It was Melchior's talent that the Jackal had craved, not Scruggs's.

Scruggs's eyes hardened. Well, he wouldn't want to be Melchior when the Master finally caught up with him. He was certain that the Jackal would have a punishment far worse than working in the brimstone mines in store for Melchior. Betrayal was the most serious of offenses. He himself had been sent down to the brimstone mines for much less. Just because he'd shown interest in a mortal woman who dealt with the Guardians occasionally, the Jackal had punished him severely. Any contact with the enemy forces, no matter how insignificant, was forbidden.

Scruggs stroked his goatee, thinking. Perhaps he could convince the Jackal to give him another chance. If he could get the boy and capture

Melchior at the same time, he might be spared another punishment in the mines. He might even be rewarded.

Hope flared in his piggish eyes. The Jackal would welcome news of Melchior's whereabouts. There were portraits of Melchior scattered throughout the Jackal's lair, promising a reward for his capture.

Scruggs walked over to the shabby wooden dresser and opened a drawer. Inside was an iron ring etched with a serpent biting its tail, just like the one Melchior had used to rescue Edward. He removed it and held it aloft for a moment. Then he spoke the ancient word, his voice taking on a gutteral growl, "*Se'ol.*"

The ring sparked as red flames danced around its edges. Moments later the inside of the ring filled with a swirling cloud. The black mist drifted in lazy circles and Scruggs could make out the dim outline of the Jackal's fortress inside the smoke. He gulped and tried to keep his face impassive as the fortress faded and was replaced by the image of an ornate throne covered with wicked barbs.

Then he saw it. The *something* that sat on that throne. A yellow eye with an icy blue pupil gazed back at him from the Oroborus. It was red-rimmed and never blinked. That eye was one of the few organic parts of the Jackal that remained. The rest of his body wheezed and clanked, bellows instead of lungs, motors where his arteries should have been. His black armor was covered with iron thorns. A long, richly embroidered cloak was fastened to his metal shoulders. A few strands of hair, once golden, but now clotted with oil and grime, hung limply from beneath his empty iron mask. The metal face had but a single hole in it, and this was the window from which his lidless orb stared. He was more machine than fallen Guardian now, but the essential parts of him that were immortal were animated by a deep, black hatred for all things good.

The Fall from the Higher Places had been dreadful for the Jackal. As he'd plummeted, the flesh had been ripped from his immortal bones while he grasped and pulled at the Seven Bridges, destroying them almost completely. It had been a cunning act of defiance. But he had paid a price for it. And gazing into that dripping, yellow orb, Whiplash Scruggs could clearly see the eternal hate that burned within the Jackal.

"You have the boy?" the Jackal wheezed. His voice was reedy and mechanical, as if it came through a flute or clarinet.

"Not yet, my Master," Whiplash Scruggs said. "But he's close," he added quickly. "He's with Melchior. I'm tracking them down even as we speak."

The eye didn't move or blink. It remained as fixed on Scruggs as if it were made of glass.

Suddenly, Whiplash Scruggs felt tremendous, searing pain course through his entire body. His hands flew to the sides of his temples and he gasped and sunk to his knees. It was a pain so horrible that it felt as if every cell in his body were about to explode. A high, clear note reverberated all around him as his internal organs were flayed from within.

A high-pitched, barking laugh like a hyena's burst from his master's lips. It was the sound that had given the Jackal his current name, the horrible laugh that sent chills down the spine of any being, mortal or immortal, that heard it. He had once been known by other, more powerful names, but the *Jackal* suited him now.

Tears slid down the sides of Scruggs's jowly cheeks. The bulky man writhed on the floor as his dogs howled in pain from their spot beneath his bed.

"Please . . . please . . ." Scruggs begged, his voice a ragged whisper. "I won't fail you again. I'll bring . . . them both to you . . . please . . ."

The high, clear note suddenly stopped. As it ended, Scruggs felt the searing pain leave his body. He lifted himself up and pulled in a deep, shuddering breath. After a moment, the Jackal spoke.

"Bring Melchior and the boy to me. Do not fail me again, Moloc."

Scruggs nodded weakly.

"Never again, my Master."

✦ Chapter Eleven ✦

ANGEL'S FLIGHT

"LOS ANGELES," the conductor's voice boomed.

Edward, who had been pretending to sleep for the last couple of hours, made a show of waking up. He yawned with exaggerated care and then glanced at Mr. Spines, who seemed not to be paying Edward any attention.

Edward felt the train begin to slow. He tried to look relaxed, as if nothing were wrong. His gaze flickered to the sliding door at the back of the coach. He'd have to be quick. To stumble or trip on his way out would cost him precious seconds. He'd had time to study the strange creature and felt pretty sure that Mr. Spines was stronger than he looked.

The gas lamps at Los Angeles Union Station flickered dully outside Edward's window. Beneath their glow, he spotted rows of canary-yellow cabs waiting to pick up arriving passengers. The taxi drivers leaned against their vehicles, chatting amiably, waiting for their next fares.

The train slowed to a crawl.

Any minute now.

"I'm starving, Melchior!" Artemis's muffled voice came from inside Mr. Spines's leather satchel. The two creatures had been placed inside so that they wouldn't attract attention when they disembarked.

"Can't we stop and get ice cream on the way to the hideout?" the toad begged.

"It's after nine o'clock; everything's closed," Spines said into the opened bag. After looking at his watch he closed its cover with a small *click*. "You can have something once we get there." He glanced up at Edward and, after noticing how pale the boy looked, offered him another of his ghastly, broken-toothed smiles.

"Don't worry about a thing, my boy. Once we get to where we're going, our troubles will be over," he said.

I doubt it, Edward thought. But he offered Spines a fake smile in return.

The train shuddered to a stop and the sound of hissing steam echoed outside the windows. Edward took a quick, deep breath.

NOW!

He was up in an instant, dashing straight to the door.

The conductor at the exit glared at him as he leaped to the ground and ran as fast as he could through the lightly crowded station. His new wings flapped behind him as he ran, and he desperately hoped that if anyone saw them that they would be mistaken for a big black overcoat. He knew that he couldn't afford to attract too much attention. Right now, all that mattered was getting away.

Far behind him he was aware of some commotion, and heard Spines's rough voice shouting, "Edward, come back!"

But he wasn't coming back. He didn't trust the misshapen creature or his strange animal sidekicks.

Edward knew that he couldn't go back to

the Foundry. He couldn't take a chance that Whiplash Scruggs was still there, and besides, he'd hated the place. No, the only option he could think of was to try to get back to Oregon and find his aunt. She was the only relative he had.

He knew that when he'd been sent to live with her after his mother died he'd been in a terrible state of mind. It was no secret that he'd acted spitefully and had withdrawn from her attempts to connect with him. But this time it would be different. He would show her that he could be well behaved. He didn't know how she would react to his new wings, but he was convinced that if he really tried, he might be able to get her to like him in spite of his strange appearance.

It was his only chance of ever having a normal home again.

At nine o'clock P.M. on a Sunday, all of the shops in Los Angeles were closed. Edward ran down the darkened streets and eventually turned down one called Alvarado. It was lined with shops built from adobe bricks, most of which were festooned with the tattered remains of colorful streamers. Glancing into some of the store windows as he ran, he saw sugar skulls grinning back at him and signs reading *DIA DE LOS MUERTOS* hung on the shop doors.

Edward had never been to California before, but if he had, he'd have understood that what he was seeing was the remains of the Mexican Day of the Dead celebration. The holiday honors loved ones who have departed, and for days the streets are decorated with flowers, candy skulls, and parades. Death is laughed at by the celebrants, and in doing so, the people accept dying as a natural part of life. The holiday was brought north into California by Mexican settlers. But Edward knew none of this. To him, the shops filled with candy skeletons and dead flowers were terrifying reminders of what he was fleeing from.

After several hundred yards, he crossed over to a deserted side street. Small, bungalow-style homes lined the road. It was less terrifying than the skeleton-themed street he'd been on before, but he still had no idea where he was.

Edward walked slowly down the deserted street, keeping to the shadows while he caught his breath. He glanced from house to house, trying desperately to think of what to do next. He wished so much that he would awake in his own bed in his mother's house to find that this was all some horrible nightmare.

As he stared longingly at the neat houses filled with happy families, something caught his eye. There was laundry hanging from a clothesline in one of the yards, and at the very end of the line was a large, black overcoat.

That's stealing, an inner voice chided. But Edward was desperate. He couldn't afford to be seen with the big, black wings growing out of his back. He might be arrested or captured and thrown into a freak show somewhere. Normally, the thought of taking something that didn't belong to him wouldn't have crossed his mind, but right now, Edward didn't feel that he had a choice.

He crept quietly into the backyard, keeping his eyes fixed on the home's windows. Anyone could see him if they happened to glance outside.

He grabbed the coat with one swift motion and dashed back out to the street. There was no sound of pursuit as he ran with the heavy bundle underneath his arm. His conscience bothered him, but he pushed it aside. He had to do whatever it took to get away from Scruggs and Spines and make it somewhere safe.

After a few blocks, Edward reached a busy intersection. He paused to put on the heavy coat and was relieved to find that it fit perfectly over his exposed wings.

Model T's raced up and down the busy road, punctuated by the light bells from cable cars. Tall buildings, bigger than any he'd seen in Portland, towered all around him. Edward stared, awestruck, at their imposing silhouettes.

As he looked around, Edward noticed a group of people waiting at a cable-car stop across the street. He felt his pockets for spare change, but knew even before he did so that he wouldn't find anything there.

He desperately wished that he'd had time to grab a few things before he'd left the Foundry. Everything had just happened so fast. And now he was in Los Angeles without any money or a place to stay. He was lost in a huge city and had no idea where to go. Suddenly everything seemed very large and terrifying. And he had no clue how he was going to get back up to Oregon with no money and no ride.

His stomach rumbled. The only thing he'd had to eat since yesterday was the shortbread cookie Spines had offered him on the train.

Okay, don't panic, he told himself. He could feel his heart racing with anxiety. *First you need to find a place to sleep for the night. Someplace safe.*

Edward walked for what seemed like hours, searching for a good place to rest. He needed a spot that was secluded enough that he wouldn't be bothered, but not far enough away from people that he couldn't call for help if he needed it. It was a scary prospect. He'd heard from his mother that Los Angeles could be dangerous place, but, until now, had never thought he'd actually be wandering its streets alone in the middle of the night.

He was glad that the overcoat he was wearing

made him look bigger and more imposing than he actually was. With his wings flattened on his back, it filled out the shoulders of the big coat and made him look older and more muscular than he really was.

Finally, after about two hours, Edward came to an unusual-looking train station. There was a big archway over a short track that extended up to the top of a hill. Situated at the bottom of the track was an elegant train made up of two cars. All the lights were off, but Edward could just make out the words written on the archway above.

ANGEL'S FLIGHT.

He looked carefully around him. The station was deserted. He moved over to the nearest car. He didn't expect it to be unlocked and was surprised when the doorknob turned easily beneath his hand.

He hazarded one more glance over his shoulder before sliding quickly inside and carefully shutting the door behind him. Inside the little car were several wooden benches.

He lay down on the nearest bench. It certainly wasn't as comfortable as a hotel room, but it was much better than sleeping in the gutter.

Edward ignored the hungry grumbling of his stomach as he pulled the big overcoat up to his neck. The hard bench was cushioned somewhat by the new wings on his back, and after scooting around a little he curled up on his side in a fairly comfortable position.

He stared into the darkness, watching as the occasional beam from a passing car's headlights illuminated his surroundings. It was hard to fall asleep in such a strange place.

As he lay there, staring into the darkness, his mind raced anxiously with possibilities, shattering his momentary feeling of safety. What if somebody showed up at the train to throw him out? What if he couldn't find a way to Oregon? Would he be stuck, living on the streets in Los Angeles? Maybe he should have just stayed with Mr. Spines.

Edward felt sick to his stomach. Whether it was from hunger or fear, he couldn't tell.

He wondered what would happen when his aunt saw his wings for the first time. Would she think he was a monster?

He rolled on his back, trying to get more comfortable. The ceiling of the train had writing scratched on it. He stared at the scrawled hearts and initials, wondering who put them there.

Edward felt a renewed surge of loneliness.

Closing his eyes, he was surprised to find that his eyelashes were wet. *No point in crying*, he thought. *Never solved anything. Nobody is here to feel sorry for you. You're on your own, just like always.*

But in spite of his best efforts, it was a very long time before the tears stopped and he finally fell asleep.

✦ Chapter Twelve ✦

HENRY AND LILITH

"Wake up, son. The conductor'll be along any minute."

Edward woke with a start to find someone shaking him gently. He sat up quickly. Beams of sunlight poured through the windows of the train, and the sounds of traffic rumbled outside. It was morning, and there were passengers on the train!

"Take it easy. We're not gonna hurt ya," said a blue-eyed older man wearing a straw boater and sporting a handlebar mustache. The man must have been who woke him. Behind him was a woman in a high-collared dress who also had pale-blue eyes and a small, pointed nose.

She indicated Edward with the point of her parasol. "What's wrong with him, Henry? Is he a mute?" she asked in a loud whisper. Edward tried to speak, but found his lips locked in a hopeless stutter.

"I-I-I w-was juh-just t-tuh-trying to guh-get some sleep," he managed. "I d-duh-didn't steal anything!"

"Nobody said you did, son," Henry said with a smile. "All I'm saying is that the conductor is on his way over, and unless you have a ticket he's probably gonna ask you to leave."

Edward's heart pounded as he saw a tall conductor taking tickets in the car in front of them. On the street outside he saw several other people waiting to board, each of them holding a small red ticket.

He stood up and was about to exit the car when the conductor noticed him. "Hey you, what do you think you're doing? Where's your ticket?"

Edward stared at his scowling face, unable to think of a reply. He stood, rooted to the spot, petrified. Suddenly he heard Henry's voice next to him say, "It's all right, Mister, he's with us. I forgot to pay at the window."

The conductor accepted the nickel that

Henry offered him with a suspicious look. Then he turned away and motioned for the others in line to board the train.

"Th-thanks," Edward mumbled gratefully. The man grinned and slapped him on the shoulder. As he did, his hand made contact with the back of Edward's wing hidden beneath the overcoat. A flash of surprise crossed Henry's face.

The train suddenly lurched forward, slowly making its way up the long hill. Henry and his wife were whispering quietly as Edward politely stared out the window. Feeling self-conscious, he adjusted the overcoat, making certain that it covered his shoulders. After a moment, Henry spoke in a casual tone.

"I guess we should introduce ourselves," Henry finally said with a grin. "My name's Henry Asmoday and this is my wife Lilith. We're down here on vacation, visiting from Salem."

Edward's heart skipped a beat as he shook the man's outstretched hand. "I'm Edward. Um, did y-you say you w-were from Salem?"

"Yep. Salem, Oregon. Prettiest little city in

the Northwest. Why d'you ask?"

Edward knew that was his chance. It was a gamble, but the people seemed honest and friendly. He didn't want to spend another terrifying night trying to sleep in Los Angeles. Maybe there was a chance that this couple could offer him a ride back up to Portland.

"I-I'm from Portland," he ventured.

"You don't say," said Henry with a look of surprise. He turned to his wife. "Well I'll be. The boy says he's from Portland, dear."

Lilith offered him a wide smile. Edward noticed that her teeth were exceptionally white and pretty. "And what are you doing so far from home, Edward?" she asked.

Edward paused before replying. He couldn't possibly tell these normal, down-to-earth people all that had happened to him in the last twenty-four hours. They would think he was insane.

He quickly thought of a lie. "I, uh, was h-here with my cousin b-but we got separated. I l-lost my train ticket home and didn't know wh-what to do."

Henry studied him quietly for a moment.

Then he said, "And what did this cousin of yours look like? Maybe we've seen him."

Edward tried to make the lie sound as convincing as he could. *Not too many details,* he warned himself. *Keep it simple.* He knew that the secret to a good lie was not to be caught up in too much elaboration. It would be too difficult for him to keep track of what he had said. And if they asked too many questions, the whole thing could fall apart.

"He's t-tall like me. Av-average looking," he said, trying to look Henry straight in the eye. As he did, he noticed how unusual the man's eyes were. They were so pale blue that they were almost colorless.

"Well, I haven't seen him," Henry said thoughtfully with a slow shake of his head. "You seen anyone like that, Lil?"

Lilith shook her head no, still giving Edward the wide smile.

"Say, I have an idea," Henry said, giving his knee a small slap. "We're heading back home this afternoon. You want to ride along with us, Edward? We've got room in the back of the car."

It was exactly what Edward had been hoping to hear. He nodded, excited by the offer.

"Th-that would be great, thanks!" he said happily.

"Let's have him for lunch," Lilith said, giving Edward an appraising look. "The poor boy looks half-starved already."

Henry nodded and grinned at him. "How 'bout it, son? Would you like to join us? We were going to have a picnic at a great spot we know of a little north of the city."

Edward couldn't believe his luck. If it hadn't been for the kindly couple coming along now, at just the right time, he would have been completely lost.

He smiled gratefully at them and said, "I c-can't thank you enough."

The train reached the top of the hill and shuddered to a stop. As the three of them stood up to exit, Lilith waved her gloved hand in a gentle motion through the air, almost as if she were conducting an invisible orchestra. Edward heard her singing a soft melody to herself. It was strange, and he couldn't be sure that he hadn't imagined it, but the air seemed to shimmer around them for the briefest second as she sang.

After finishing the light tune, she turned to her husband and smiled.

"Let's hit the road. I'm starving."

✦ Chapter Thirteen ✦

HARP

"I can't smell him anymore," Sariel said. The ermine had her nose close to the sidewalk at the top of the hill, just outside the deserted Angel's Flight train station.

"He was here recently, I'm sure of it. But it's like he completely disappeared. There's no scent at all."

Mr. Spines rubbed his forehead anxiously. It had taken all last night and most of the day to track the boy all the way from Union station.

Spines knew that Los Angeles could be a dangerous place for mortals. The crime-ridden streets weren't anything like the tranquil Oregon logging towns, most of which were filled with simple country folk. But it wasn't the mortal dangers that worried him about Los Angeles. It was the capital city for the Jackal's forces, and that made it a deadly place for Guardians to visit. Groundlings were everywhere, masquerading as humans. If one of them discovered what Edward was, the boy didn't stand a chance.

A flapping of wings caused him to look up. Artemis soared into view, his bulky form silhouetted against the late-afternoon sun.

"Well?" Spines asked.

"Nothing, sir," Artemis said breathlessly. The big toad flopped to the ground. "I must have followed a dozen trolley cars but none of them had Edward inside of them. Oooh," he moaned. "I've never had to fly so far with these stupid reptile wings. They feel like they're gonna fall off."

"Well maybe if you weren't stuffing your face all the time, you'd have had an easier time of it," Sariel said, shooting Artemis an imperious look. "It's no wonder I'm the one that has to do everything around here. You're useless."

"Well, you're nothing but a stuck-up sewer rat," Artemis fired back. "You should see how ugly you look. At least I can lose weight."

"Take it back!"

"Make me!"

Mr. Spines paced in front of the train station, trying to ignore the heated exchange between his two apprentices. Since the Fall, Sariel had grown increasingly arrogant, and Artemis was a glutton. The Corruption was working its slow poison. They couldn't avoid the Jackal's influences forever. If Spines's plan with Edward failed, they would all soon turn into full-fledged Groundlings. They would lose their ability to feel anything but the same twisted feelings of revenge and hatred that motivated the Jackal. Every thought would be a desire to inflict harm rather than to protect. The flickering candle of good that still burned in their hearts would be snuffed out forever.

Mr. Spines sighed and scratched his stubbly cheek. The situation with Edward was more serious than he had feared. The fact that his scent had gone cold could mean only one thing. Groundlings were experts at avoiding detection. If one of them had Edward and didn't want anyone to follow, they could erase any sign that they'd ever been there. There was only one way to track Edward now, and Spines was reluctant to use it.

He stared up at the long stretch of railroad tracks that led up the hill and faded into the darkness, thinking about the price of what he was about to do. He was a fallen Guardian, and Songs of Power were forbidden to him now. This was because, for a Guardian, a Song of Power was magic itself. It could do anything from finding a lost treasure to fortifying the singer with magical armor. Simple tunes did simple things, but there was a higher sort of song, called an Aria, that took a lifetime to master and could accomplish tremendous feats of power.

That was why the Jackal had forbidden all of the Guardians' songs. And the penalty for singing them was proportional to the power of the song. If a fallen Guardian sung an Aria, it would release a wave of corruption so tremendous that the singer could die a very painful death.

But Melchior wasn't even sure that his voice could sing one anymore. The consequence of botching up a song that was as powerful as he intended to sing was terrible. He could get away with singing the simple ones in his corrupted state, but to sing an Aria in his fallen form was nothing short of suicidal.

He fidgeted with his pocket watch, opening and closing the lid repeatedly with several sharp *clicks*. Then, after a long moment, he turned to Sariel and said quietly, "I need my harp."

Sariel's eyes widened. "You can't be serious."

Spines sighed. "You heard what I said, young one."

Artemis and Sariel exchanged a nervous glance. Their master had not used his harp since the Fall. He had told them repeatedly how dangerous it would be to use it and had warned them never to touch it.

"But Melchior," Artemis whined. "You said we shouldn't—"

"I know exactly what I said, Artemis," Mr. Spines said firmly. "But this is what must be done. It's the only way." Mr. Spines reached into his jacket pocket and pulled out a small sphere.

The sphere was made of perfectly smooth wood. On the top of the globe was a strange-looking letter, Melchior's Guardian symbol, burned into its surface. Mr. Spines raised the globe and spoke an ancient word.

"*Sisma.*"

A golden seam appeared around the circumference of the wooden ball. Then the two halves suddenly split open, revealing something that looked like a tiny, glowing pebble hidden inside of it. Mr. Spines carefully removed the glowing speck. He raised it to his stubbly lips and breathed on it. The pebble glowed brightly for a moment before fading. Then the magical stone changed shape, growing into something strange and wonderful. Where the tiny speck of light had been sitting before was now an ornately carved, compact harp.

Spines lifted the instrument and gave the strings an experimental strum. A sound like a beautiful chorus of birds filled the air on the darkened city street.

Still in tune, he mused. The ermine and the toad looked on, their eyes wide with apprehension.

"I'm going to try to sing the Song of

Retrieval," Spines began, his fingers moving gently up and down the harp strings. "It will summon a hunter who will track Edward down. When it appears, you must get on its back and hold on. Don't let go! If you lose your grip and fall off, the hunter will disappear and there's no way I'll be able to summon it again."

He reached into a pouch at his belt and handed Sariel the Oroborus.

"Use this if you have to defend yourselves. I don't know where Edward is or what's happened to him, but I fear the worst. After you set him free, meet me back at the house on Bunker Hill."

"But you're coming with us, right?" Artemis asked anxiously.

Spines lowered the harp and gave him a serious look. "I'll have to stay here and give the song its power. I won't stop singing until the hunter gives me the signal that he's found the boy." He hesitated before continuing. "I may not see you again. As I've told you before, the consequences for singing a forbidden song are serious."

Both creatures nodded gravely. They knew

that what their master was about to do could destroy him, and they felt terrified at the prospect of losing him. Melchior was the closest thing to a father the two creatures had. They had been only minor Guardians when they fell, and were still young.

Spines knelt down beside them and gave each of them a slight embrace. "It's not over yet," he said. "If there weren't any hope, then I wouldn't be doing this."

The two creatures nodded silently again, like small children being reassured by a loving parent. Mr. Spines smiled gently and rose to his feet. He lifted the harp and began working his fingers back and forth along the strings.

Once again, beautiful notes filled the air around them. Melchior smiled, feeling a surge of joy in spite of the fearfully dangerous thing he was about to do. It had been too long since he'd made this kind of music. He hadn't realized until now just how much he missed being a Guardian.

If it hadn't been for *her*, he would still be in the Woodbine. He would still be a Guardian.

Had it been worth it? He glanced at the small band of white gold that encircled the index finger of his left hand. Yes, it had been worth it. He knew it without a doubt. He would have done it again a thousand times over.

But the most important thing now was that *she* needed him to get the boy. The boy was the key to everything.

A silvery glow built around the strings as the powerful melody took form. Spines closed his eyes, allowing the magic to flow into his heart and mind. He could tell right away that it was going to be a struggle. He could feel the pure music traveling from his fingertips to his wrists and up into his arms. But once there, the flow met resistance. It was like a bubbling spring trying desperately to push its way into a fetid swamp. He could feel the purity fighting against the black fluid of corruption that filled his veins.

You can do this. He gritted his teeth. He felt the pain start to build in his forearms. His fingers burned but he forced them to continue to strum the silver strings. *It won't last forever,* he assured himself. *I just have to keep playing no matter what happens.*

Then he lifted his head to the stars and began to sing.

✦ Chapter Fourteen ✦
DINNER

Edward sat in the back of the Model A Ford, enjoying the luxurious feel of the leather seat beneath him as they puttered down the busy Los Angeles street. He gazed outside of the small, glass window to the beautiful buildings and the newly planted palm trees, glad to finally be heading home.

Henry and Lilith had offered him a piece of saltwater taffy to chew on the way to their picnic. He was enjoying the cool sweetness, happy for the first time in ages. He was on his way back to Oregon. Everything was going to work out all right. No more Foundry, no more Scruggs, no more Spines, and no more running. He would get to his aunt and explain what had happened and everything would be sorted out.

"How you doing back there, Ed?

Comfortable?" Henry called back over his shoulder.

"Yeah, great!" Edward said without the slightest hint of a stutter. "This is sure a neat car. I've never been in one like this before!"

"She's a beaut all right," Henry said proudly. "I bought her off some rube down in Santa Monica for a song. The chump didn't know what he had." He patted the dashboard affectionately. "She might be a few years old, but she still runs like a champ."

"How much farther to the picnic spot?" Edward asked eagerly. It seemed like they'd been driving forever. He'd finished the taffy and was starting to feel really hungry.

"Won't be too long," Lilith said, flashing him a grin. "Just sit back and enjoy the ride. We'll be there soon."

The sun was already well on its way to going down when they finally stopped at a huge park on the outskirts of the city. Edward was starving. They had driven for what seemed like hours! Edward glanced outside the window at the park. It had a beautiful lake in its center and was surrounded on all sides by tall, waving palm trees.

"Here we are," Henry said, pulling back the brake. "Echo Park."

Edward got out of the car and gazed around appreciatively. Henry and Lilith were right. It definitely was a beautiful spot for a picnic, especially at sunset. "It's really nice. We don't have palm trees in Oregon," he called back over his shoulder.

He felt Henry and Lilith approach, standing on either side of his shoulders. Glancing up, he noticed that they were staring directly at him, with strange, fixed smiles, their pale blue eyes shining in the waning light.

"So, when do we eat?" Edward asked, feeling uncomfortable. He looked around and noticed that neither of them seemed to be holding a picnic basket. "Uh . . . W-What's for dinner?"

Henry and Lilith shared a laugh. The tall woman put a hand on Edward's shoulder and her smile widened. Edward noticed again that she had very white teeth, but this time he noticed something else about them. Something that he hadn't seen the first time that they met. It was a subtle thing, something that gave her smile an unusual twist.

They were very, very sharp.

✦ Chapter Fifteen ✦
HUNTER

The song that Melchior sang was imperfect and raw. Had he possessed the vocal cords he once had, it would have soared with the power of a fifty-piece orchestra. In comparison, the best he could do now was what sounded to his ears like an out-of-tune string quartet. But by any mortal standards, it was beautiful.

Each note struck upon his harp harmonized with Melchior's deep voice, filling the melody with rich overtones. The effect it produced on Sariel and Artemis was instantaneous. It had been a long time since they'd heard the powerful music of the Woodbine, and it immediately inspired feelings of courage inside both of their hearts.

As the beautiful harmonies wove a tapestry of song, several shining circles materialized on the ground in front of them. At first, they looked like four glowing teacups turned upside down. But then the cups spouted thick, heavy stalks growing up from the center of each one. The stalks grew taller and joined in the middle, thickening into a wide body. It was at that moment that Sariel and Artemis realized what they were seeing. With a thrill, they realized that it was the body of a horse, growing from its hooves upward.

They gazed in amazement as the horse's chestnut body sprouted a long, golden tail. Then, instead of the neck and head that they expected to see rise out of the horse's trunk, something else emerged instead.

It was the upper torso of a powerfully built man with a quiver of arrows slung over his shoulder. His huge right hand held a bow made of bronze and his face was ferocious and strong.

Beads of sweat appeared on Melchior's forehead as he continued to play and sing, the melody changing to sound like a hunting horn. The gigantic centaur, for that is what it was, blinked slowly and raised its bearded face to the sky, listening closely to the lyrics of the song. Then, after a moment, its expression hardened into a sense of purpose. The lyrics in the song had told it exactly what it was supposed to do.

Sariel and Artemis were so taken by the magical creature and the song that they almost forgot their mission. Sariel felt that she could have stayed for hours, just listening to the beautiful music. Her eyes traveled from the centaur to her master's face. Melchior's expression was determined, but his hands shook as they strummed the harp strings. Singing the forbidden song was taking every ounce of strength he had. It was then that she suddenly remembered her master's instructions. They were supposed to jump on the centaur's back!

"Quick, get on!" she shouted to Artemis, feeling angry at herself for delaying. She scurried up the creature's massive foreleg, knowing full well that they didn't have any time to lose.

"Oh!" Artemis said, blinking. Then he quickly hopped into the air and flapped up behind where Sariel sat perched upon the creature's back.

Sariel glanced over at Melchior again and immediately wished she hadn't. Her master's face had turned chalky white. Porcupine quills like the ones he had beneath his hat were now sprouting on his arms and legs. He was covered with a coat of thorns, and as each new quill shot out of his skin, a spasm of pain crossed his face.

She knew at once what it was.

The Corruption.

It was the thing that had been at work on them all since they fell, the terrible curse that the Jackal put on all of his servants.

She'd watched, horrified, the first time the curse had taken effect. Shortly after the Fall, she, Melchior, and Artemis had started to change. The first stages of the Corruption had been subtle. But over the succeeding months she had begun to shrink, growing more and more fur. It was quicker for Artemis and her, for they were low-ranking Guardians and didn't possess as much resistance as Melchior. But she could never forget the horror as she made the painful transformation from a beautiful Guardian into an animal. It had been terrible to watch her human body and glossy wings disappear before her very eyes.

With a sick feeling in the pit of her stomach, she wondered what would be left of Mr. Spines when she saw him again.

But there was no time to ponder this. The magical Hunter had received the instructions that Spines had woven into his song. The melody had spoken to him of the tall boy with ebony wings, and the magical creature knew immediately what to do and where to find him.

With a lurch, the huge centaur bounded into the dusky Los Angeles street, taking off at a blazing gallop. The tiny ermine gripped his flanks as tightly as she could with her paws, her hair and whiskers flying behind her.

"Hang on!" she shouted back to Artemis, whose toad eyes were bulging with fear. He had his webbed fingers wrapped tightly around her middle.

"Whatever you do, don't let go!"

✦ Chapter Sixteen ✦

ECHO PARK

"Stay away from me!" Edward shouted as he backed slowly toward the murky water, clutching his bleeding arm. The sun had sunk below the mountains, and, in the encroaching darkness, Echo Park had undergone a transformation. The shadows cast by the swaying palms resembled long arms with claw-like hands. The glittering water of the lake had turned into an impenetrable swamp. And Henry and Lilith, the innocent tourists from Salem, Oregon, had become something else. They bared their sharp, pointy teeth in animalistic grins and were advancing slowly, like lions circling some wounded prey. They looked very, very hungry.

"Now, now Edward. I told you we weren't gonna hurt ya," Henry said, his pale eyes glinting in the semi-darkness. Lilith chuckled. "That's right," she added. "But I'm sure that the Jackal won't mind if we have just one more little bite before we send you to meet him." She gazed at Edward's skinny arm with greedy anticipation. Her voice took on a whimpering, desperate tone. "The fingers this time, Asmoday. He won't be needing *them*."

Edward heard a sucking sound beneath his feet and looked down. To his horror he realized that he'd backed into the muddy bank at the edge of the lake. There was nowhere left for him to run and he didn't know how to swim well enough to get across the lake. Plus, he doubted that he could outswim Henry and Lilith, even if he did know how!

Lilith swiped at him, narrowly missing his arm. Edward jerked backward at the last second. She laughed as he teetered at the edge of the water, his long arms rotating like a windmill as he tried to regain his balance.

"Look at him, Henry!" the woman cackled. "He looks like a scarecrow!"

Suddenly, from somewhere deep inside of him, a new awareness washed over Edward as he looked into the hungry faces of Henry and Lilith. He stared at them, seeing what they were for the very first time.

They weren't human at all. They were something else.

Something evil.

Then, like the moment in the cellar when he'd needed it most, a new word came unbidden to his lips. He didn't know why, but he shouted the strange word as it rushed into his mind, putting everything he had into it.

"HISTALEK!"

The scent of burning ozone filled the air.

Then suddenly, tremendous bolts of blue lightning shot from each of Edward's outstretched hands. There was barely time for Henry and Lilith to react. Their faces registered shock as the crackling surges of electricity snaked through the air and slammed into each of their chests.

Lilith screamed.

BOOM! The earth shook as the couple was catapulted backward. Seconds later, their two smoking, twisted bodies hit the hard-packed ground thirty yards away with sickening *thuds*!

Edward stood at the edge of the lake, unable to believe what he'd just seen. Every ounce of strength had left his body. His knees were quivering so badly, he could barely stand. How had he done that?

In the distance, the crumpled forms of Henry and Lilith began to move. Their bodies jerked slowly upward, like marionettes being pulled awkwardly to their feet. Edward stared, horrified at the wisps of gray smoke trailing upward from their charred skin. After a blast of lightning like that, he thought that they would have been dead for sure! Nothing human could have survived that.

"Guardian," Lilith hissed at Edward, her voice sounding as ragged as she looked. "You have made a grave mistake."

He'd never thought of himself as a Guardian before. But he didn't have time to ponder this. Instead, he watched, horrified, as Lilith's smile stretched, becoming a long, terrible jaw riddled with needlelike teeth.

Henry Asmoday howled, a roar that echoed

through the abandoned park. It was a single, prolonged shout full of hate.

"KILLLLLLLLLLL!"

The nice gentleman Edward met at the train station had long disappeared. Now Henry Asmoday's hair smoked from the lightning blast and his terrible fangs were bared in a vicious smile. Edward noticed that Henry's pale, icy blue eyes glinted with malice—eyes that wanted nothing more than to see him die.

And suddenly Edward realized that he'd seen eyes like that many times before. His least favorite teachers at the Foundry, Miss Polanski and Mr. Ignatius, had had them. His aunt's lawyer had had them, too. Whiplash Scruggs, Lilith, and Henry all had them. It suddenly seemed as if those eyes were everywhere he'd ever been. Watching him. Waiting for an opportunity. Waiting to destroy him.

He'd never been more terrified than he felt at that moment. Henry and Lilith were closing in on him, but Edward was too weak from the tremendous burst of energy he'd expelled to fight back.

Let it be quick, he prayed.

Suddenly, a burning ring of fire shot through the air, embedding itself neatly into Asmoday's exposed side. The man howled in pain, stumbled, and fell into the lake beside Edward with a tremendous splash.

Edward glanced up, unable to believe his eyes. A huge, galloping centaur carrying something that looked like a white weasel and a flying toad had thundered into view. He realized it was Sariel and Artemis.

"Get on!" the white animal shouted.

Edward didn't need to be asked twice. In spite of his weak and shaking arms, he managed to climb onto the centaur's back.

They were about to leave when suddenly he felt something heavy grip his ankle. One of Lilith's clawlike hands had grabbed the bottom of his leg and was pulling him from the centaur's back.

"Help!" he cried.

The centaur immediately responded, pulling a long arrow from the quiver on his back. A split-second later, the arrow was embedded in one of Lilith's horrible blue eyes.

"AIIIIIIEEEEEEE!" Her unearthly scream echoed around them as Edward felt the woman's grip slip from his leg.

"GO!" shouted Sariel.

"But what about the Oroborus?" shouted Artemis, looking at Asmoday, who had recovered and was rising out of the water. The blazing ring was still embedded in his side.

"We have to leave it!" Sariel shouted. Her tiny fists pounded on the centaur's shoulder. "Take us to the hideout!"

The centaur reared back and then lurched forward. He loosed an arrow as he ran, sending the shaft skyward in an explosion of golden sparks that lit up the night sky. It was the signal he had been commanded to send when he had accomplished his task.

Far away, Melchior saw the tiny shower of sparks and lowered the harp. The Song of Retrieval was complete.

"Safe," he whispered, relieved.

His face was deathly pale. New spines pierced through the back of his coat and trouser legs. He was more shrunken and twisted than he'd ever been.

His breathing was labored and he knew walking would be difficult. The Corruption had taken a severe toll.

At least I'm not dead, he thought. But then he heard a voice behind him that made him wonder if death might have been preferable.

"Hello, Melchior," the voice said with a distinctly southern drawl.

✦ Chapter Seventeen ✦

THE BRADBURY

The Jackal's headquarters was housed in an elegant building known to Angelinos as the Bradbury Building. It was a massive feat of engineering, with tall columns and twisted iron filigree, but the true wonder was that the mortal citizens of Los Angeles always failed to notice the one thing that unified the Bradbury's many residents. Each of the policeman, lawyers, doctors, and businessmen that traversed its narrow corridors had one unique attribute in common. They all had eyes that were such a pale blue they were almost colorless.

At the very bottom floor of the Bradbury Building was a basement used for storage. In the far corner of that basement, hidden behind a bunch of unused filing cabinets, was a door. Behind the door and down a long flight of stairs was Whiplash Scruggs's favorite place: the torture chamber.

It was to here that the bulky man dragged the pitiful body of Mr. Spines. He was chained and thrown into a crumbling brick cell to wait for whatever was in store for him next. Mr. Spines drifted in and out of consciousness.

He wasn't sure how long he had been there when he woke with a terrible thirst, but there was nothing to drink. He'd tried to sip a few drops of rusty water that leaked from the slime-ridden pipes on the wall, but had given that up quickly. Like everything else in the Jackal's earthly headquarters, it was foul and poisonous.

Spines knew that the Corruption was close to completion. If he didn't get the help he needed, he would be transformed into a full-fledged Groundling. He would become a creature that was entirely of the same mind as the Jackal, filled with hatred for all things good and true.

Unfortunately, the cure he needed was nowhere to be found on Earth. He needed a choir of Guardians to sing the *Chorus of Restoration*, a powerful melody that had to be sung by no fewer than twelve for its magical healing power to work. His only chance for healing was in the Woodbine, the one place forbidden to him now, and the place he needed to get to more than anywhere else.

Mr. Spines was startled to hear heavy footsteps echoing outside his moldy cell and then a key turn the rusty lock on his door. He understood what would be coming next. But no matter how much he was tortured, he was determined not to tell Scruggs what he desperately wanted to know.

Edward's location would remain secret at any cost.

✦ Chapter Eighteen ✦

HIDEOUT

"But where is he? I thought he said he was going to meet us here?" Artemis whined. He was still shaken up from their encounter with the Groundlings in Echo Park. Luckily for them, the centaur had been able to whisk them to Spines's secret hideout with lightning speed. Right after he had delivered them to the front door, he'd faded from view with a triumphant blast of his hunting horn.

Artemis hated to think what would have happened if they had been forced to confront the two Groundlings in open battle.

"He'll be here, don't worry," the ermine said.

Sariel scurried over to the wall and turned on the gas lamps in the elegant living room. Artemis could tell from her voice that she wasn't confident.

"What is this p-place?" Edward asked, noticing the richly carved mahogany furniture with satin pillows. On the high walls were portraits of dignified gentlemen that stared down at him with haughty expressions. Edward had never been in such a luxurious house. He couldn't help feeling like an intruder and wondered if they really had permission to be there.

"We're in a house in Bunker Hill's most exclusive neighborhood. An unlikely spot for a group of fallen Guardians, I know, but we got lucky. Melchior has a generous benefactor." Sariel hopped onto a sitting chair and indicated a portrait on the wall. Edward observed a stodgy-looking gentleman with bushy sideburns and glasses.

"That's Prudent Beaudry. He was the mayor of Los Angeles about thirty or forty years ago. His family wanted to know how their grandfather was doing in the Afterlife and Melchior found out for them. In return, they allow us to use his house as a base of operations when we're stupid enough to come down here," Artemis said bitterly. "But that's probably going to change now that you had to go and get caught up with the two of *them*."

"Wh-what do you m-mean?" Edward asked.

"Don't you know who we rescued you from back there in the park?" Artemis asked, fixing Edward with a pointed stare. Edward shook his head "no."

"It was Asmoday and Lilith—two of the most feared Groundlings in the Jackal's army!" The toad sounded almost hysterical. "If it hadn't been for Sariel's shot with the Oroborus, Asmoday would have killed you."

The toad let out a pitiful moan, grabbing his head with his webbed hands. "I can't stand this anymore," he complained. "Why did Melchior force us to come down here? We were doing just fine up in Portland."

"You know why," Sariel said. She glanced up at Edward. "We're just going to have to make the best of it until Melchior gets here. Then we'll be going to 'you know where.'"

"I want to know w-what's going on around here," Edward said firmly. "Everybody kuh-keeps talking l-like I'm not even here. T-tell me the plan or I'm n-not going with you."

Sariel and Artemis shared a look.

"We're only trying to help you, Edward. You've got to trust us," Sariel said in a pleading voice.

"Why sh-should I?" he said, his eyes flashing angrily. "You nuh-never even asked me if I-I wanted to come with you. You didn't even introduce y-yourselves. You just sh-showed up and grabbed me at the Foundry. Then you k-keep hinting th-that we're going somewhere and that it's dangerous. I deserve to know whu-what's going on."

He glared down at her with his arms crossed.

Sariel looked back up at him for a long moment. Then after glancing at Edward's bloody sleeve she sighed and said, "First let me get you a bandage for your arm. Then I'll tell you what I can."

The bite he'd sustained from Lilith wasn't deep, but it was raw and dirty. Edward winced as the ermine applied soap and water to the wound and began dressing it with a clean linen bandage.

The ordeal with Henry and Lilith had been terrifying. He'd never expected to be attacked by such normal-seeming people.

Sariel spoke, interrupting his thoughts. "Okay, so what do you want to know first?"

Edward's eyes narrowed. "You told me on the train that the three of you had *fallen* from that place, what did you call it?" Edward thought for a moment, trying to remember the name. "The Wildbrine or something. How do I know that you're not evil and that you have some secret plan to kill me or something? Those other two guys seemed trustworthy and then they turned out to be deranged monsters."

Sariel chuckled as she tightened the last part of the linen cloth and secured it. "First of all, the place you're talking about is called the *Woodbine*." She glanced up at Edward with a serious expression. "And as far as being 'evil' goes, I don't really know how to answer that. I guess you could say that we made a serious mistake. But the major difference between us and the Groundlings is that we didn't fall because we wanted to serve the Jackal. We all fell for a completely different reason." Sariel's voice trailed off and she gazed out of the window for a long moment.

Edward noticed her sudden shift in attitude and asked, "Well, how c-come they all look human and y-you don't?"

Sariel sighed and said, "In the Woodbine, things take on the appearance of what they truly are on the inside. When a Guardian falls, he or she is changed. Most of the Groundlings are vain creatures, and crave the physical beauty they once possessed. The Jackal uses his power on those who serve him most faithfully. He gives them a kind of shell that masks most of the changes." She shrugged. "All except for the eyes and teeth, that is. You probably noticed that."

Edward nodded, thinking of Lilith and Henry's terrible gaze. He shuddered to think that they served a master who was even more powerfully evil than they were.

Sariel continued, "He also invented something called the Corruption. The Jackal uses it as a way to control his servants. Whenever a Groundling does something that is in direct disobedience to one of his laws, they undergo a painful transformation." She indicated her back. "That's why my wings shrank. I once sang a Song of Power to try to force one of the Groundlings' Oroboruses to function like a Guardian's Ring." She shuddered. "It really hurt. The Jackal's weapons are designed only for his evil purposes," she said. "And because I tried to alter it, I was punished."

Changing the subject, Edward asked, "But you s-still haven't told me why I'm here. You say you d-don't serve the Jackal, so what is it you w-want with me? I d-don't understand what this is all about."

Sariel looked uncomfortable. She and Artemis exchanged nervous glances. Edward could tell that they weren't going to give him a straight answer. He scowled and said, "I'm guessing that Mr. Spines has told you that you can't tell me exactly why."

Sariel nodded and offered him a wistful smile. "I'm sure he'll tell you eventually. After all, she was your mother . . ."

Sariel suddenly clapped her tiny hands to her

mouth with a look of horror.

"You weren't supposed to tell!" Artemis shouted. "Wonderful. Now Melchior's really going to get us in trouble," he added gloomily.

Edward sat back on the couch with a stunned expression. "I d-don't understand. What does this have to do with my mother?" he demanded.

"Well, it's just that, um . . . you see, it's not just about your mother, really . . . it's just . . ." the ermine wrung her hands fretfully.

"You might as well tell him. It's too late now, anyway," Artemis said bitterly. Turning to Edward, he said, "Melchior invented a machine that can take us back to the Woodbine. It's ingenious! Until he came up with it there was no way for a fallen Guardian to get back there. Well, that is, unless they were servants of the Jackal, of course," Artemis added.

Edward listened with rapt attention.

The toad fluttered up onto the coffee table in front of the couch and continued. "The reason we came for you is that your mother is up there and we need your help to rescue her. She's been captured and imprisoned in the Jackal's fortress.

I know we should have told you, but Melchior wanted to tell you in his own time."

Edward's head was spinning. He felt his new wings press softly into his back as he slumped into the back cushion of the couch. His mother was still alive? But how could she be? She was dead! He'd watched helplessly as cancer had ravaged her body, stealing her away from him. It had been the most traumatic experience of his life.

He stared at Artemis with a dumbfounded expression. Could it possibly be true? Hope suddenly flared in his chest. There was nothing, absolutely nothing, he wouldn't have given to get to see his mother one last time. And if she were in danger he didn't care where it was, he would do whatever it took to find her.

"Show me how to get there."

"What?" asked Sariel.

"To the Woodbine. I want to see my mother." Edward wore a determined expression.

"But we can't go yet. We need Melchior, he's the only one who knows how to operate the machine."

"Okay then, take me to the machine," Edward said. He removed the pack of tattered playing cards from his back pocket.

"I want to see it."

✦ Chapter Nineteen ✦

LAIR

"He is being difficult, Master," Scruggs said, bowing low before the Jackal's throne. "If I had a little more time I'm sure I could get him to tell me where the boy is hidden."

Scruggs kept his gaze locked on the floor, afraid to look into the Jackal's terrible eye. He'd been summoned to the lair and he knew what it meant. A private audience with the Jackal was never good.

The Jackal's yellow orb remained fixed on Whiplash Scruggs for a long moment. Then, with a loud wheeze, the bellows inside his mechanical chest began to inflate. "Melchior has reason to be stubborn, Moloc," the Jackal said in a reedy voice. "A father will go to great lengths to protect his son. He will die before he tells us where the boy is hidden." There was a pause while the bellows inflated again. "Allow Melchior to escape and then track him to the boy. Take fifty Groundlings with you. I don't . . . *sssssssss.*" There was a hissing sound as the Jackal's mechanical lungs ran out of air. After a pause to refill his bellows, his reedy voice continued, ". . . want any mistakes this time, Moloc. You didn't capture the boy on your last mission. This is your one and only chance to redeem yourself."

Whiplash Scruggs knew that he'd been granted a reprieve. Failing the Jackal twice didn't happen often.

As he strode from the Jackal's chamber, he cursed his luck. He'd hoped to finish torturing Melchior. Being forced to allow him to escape filled Scruggs with disgust.

The click of his boot heels echoed down the dank corridors as he stomped along. Groundlings of all shapes and sizes, all of them corrupted and twisted according to the Jackal's whims, swarmed through the passages. Most of them were on assignment, working to torment their mortal victims on Earth.

Later, he thought as he weaved through the throng of bodies. *After I deliver the boy to the Jackal, I'll reward myself with something extra special for Melchior.*

He smiled. There were many tortures he'd been waiting to try out for centuries.

✦ Chapter Twenty ✦
LIBERTY

The rusted chains on Mr. Spines's wrists bit deep into his flesh, but he hardly noticed them. They were nothing compared to the scores of lash marks that had turned his back to ribbons. Scruggs had spared no mercy when applying his whip, and Melchior knew that his strength was running out. He had to find a way to escape soon or he'd be too weak to try.

He gazed around the gloomy prison, noting the heavy iron grates that covered every exit. There was only one way he knew of to break through iron.

He hesitated, wondering if he had the strength to attempt another forbidden song. He had taken such songs for granted when he was a Guardian. "Broken Chains" was an elementary tune for any young Guardian, but to sing it now, in his corrupt condition, was to take a substantial risk. Fortunately it was a short song, only one quick verse. The longer Songs of Power required more time to sing, and with them came a longer exposure to the Corruption.

Must try, he told himself, gathering his strength. He took a deep breath and was instantly rewarded with spasms of intense pain.

This was going to be difficult.

He closed his eyes to keep the room from spinning. After a few seconds he was ready to try again. This time he drew his breath very slowly, and although it still hurt, he was able to hold it.

He exhaled and his voice rose, softly at first, but more loudly as the song went on. The lyrics to the song weren't difficult, but the cadence of the melody was tricky. It was almost a chant, sounding something like the blows of a blacksmith's hammer as he shaped a piece of metal.

After the first stanza, Mr. Spines could feel the rusted chains that held his hands and feet begin to weaken. He struggled against the Corruption that threatened to overwhelm him once more.

Hang on. Just a little more. He increased the volume of his song, giving it all the remaining strength he possessed.

CREAK! The chains groaned under the force of the powerful song. It took all of Melchior's strength not to scream as new quills sprouted out of his wounded back. As the song continued, all of the iron in the horrible chamber showed signs of weakening. The iron portcullis that covered the exits began to bend and twist. Rivets popped and finally, with a resounding *CRACK!* the manacles on Mr. Spines's feet and wrists completely fell away.

He rose shakily from the table, barely able to stand. The toll that the song had taken on him wasn't quite as severe as the last song, but he was severely wounded and needed medical attention.

Not long and I'll be back in the Woodbine, he reassured himself.

As he limped to the chamber exit, he thought longingly of the medicine he'd brought with him from the Woodbine, a special concoction he kept in a cabinet at the hideout. Even though it wouldn't do much about the Corruption, it would help to heal his ragged back.

Because his mind was distracted by the terrible pain, he didn't notice that neither Whiplash Scruggs nor any of the Groundlings were around to stop his exit. Under normal circumstances he would have been immediately suspicious. But all he could focus on as he ascended the long flight of stairs that led to the ground floor of the building above was a single thought, which he repeated over and over in his mind.

Help the boy. Find his mother.

✦ Chapter Twenty-One ✦
MACHINE

When Edward walked up the stairs and opened the door to the attic of Mr. Spines's hideout, he gasped as the door swung open and revealed a room filled with marvels.

Where the wooden roof had once been, Spines had created a ceiling of stained glass that held illustrations of fantastic creatures. Edward stared at the panes of colorful glass, marveling at the pictures of gigantic blue snails with elderly, human faces. Green-skinned warriors hefting spears rode on their spiral shells. Beneath the incredible ceiling was a huge, clockwork machine made of brass and steel that rotated slowly, powered by hidden motors. Stretching outward from its base were long metal arms that cradled spinning models of planets.

It was an incredible laboratory, the likes of

which would have made Mr. Jules Verne himself turn green with envy.

Eventually, Edward's eyes fell on a machine in the corner that looked like a large telephone booth covered with gauges and dials. Hoses snaked out from the sides of the cabinet, ending at a huge boiler tank. Little bursts of steam shot from hidden valves, reminding Edward of a toy train engine.

"That's it over there," Sariel said nervously. She looked guilty. "We probably shouldn't stay up here long. Melchior wouldn't want us to linger."

Edward ignored her and walked directly over to the machine. He scanned its incredibly intricate machinery, trying to figure out how it worked. He noticed a large, glass capsule filled with golden fluid that was attached to its side by a brass fitting. Upon closer inspection, he saw tiny measurement lines painted on its side, indicating that the fluid level was at the top.

What's that for? he wondered. He brushed the innumerable gauges, buttons, and switches with his fingertips, wishing that one of them had the words *off* and *on* written on it.

"You shouldn't touch those," Artemis said. "Melchior's the only one who knows exactly how to work it."

"I agree," Sariel added. "Let's go. We've been here long enough."

"One second," said Edward. He moved a crate of machine parts out of the way and knelt down on the wooden floor. Then he opened the pack of cards and started to build. As he put each card into place, he felt the familiar sense of calm rush over him, and his mind began to clear. Suddenly he found that he could picture the machine in perfect detail, including the size and relationship of every switch, knob, and button.

Okay, he thought. *Three green buttons on the top, a yellow switch next to those, a gauge marked "Pressure" underneath that . . .*

There is a secret language that inventors and engineers are born with. It's an unspoken thing, an understanding that helps them decide how and why things are put together in certain ways. This knowledge flooded into Edward's mind with stunning clarity as he constructed his card house.

It was as if he could suddenly understand exactly how Mr. Spines had built it.

Edward set down the last card on top of the house's roof and stood up.

"Edward, what is it? What are you doing?" Fear was in Sariel's voice as she watched Edward move over to the panel of colored buttons.

He knew exactly what to do.

Melchior hobbled up to the front steps of the Victorian house. His breath came in ragged gasps as he approached the door.

"Not yet," cautioned Whiplash Scruggs in a hushed voice. "Wait until I give the signal." His Groundling lieutenant crouched in the bushes beside him, eager to send his fifty soldiers after the renegade Guardian.

"Yesss, Commander," the Groundling hissed. The terrifying creature had the head of a serpent and the body of a bat-winged lion. It fingered a rusted Oroborus at its belt with its long-nailed fingers, anticipating the attack.

Mr. Spines was unaware that he was being

followed. He stumbled into the house and after looking around and seeing nobody, called, "Sariel! Artemis! Edward! Are you here?"

No response. "Where are they?" Spines muttered. *Did something go wrong with the rescue attempt?* His back hurt terribly. He needed to get upstairs to the lab and retrieve his healing elixir.

CRAAACK! A huge noise, like the sound of lightning striking a tree, ripped through the air. It was followed by the distinct smell of ozone.

"No!" Spines shouted. In spite of the terrible pain he was in, he rushed up the stairs to the attic and burst through the door to his laboratory. The sight that met his eyes almost made him faint.

Sariel and Artemis stood in front of the smoking machine, gazing at him with helpless, terrified expressions.

"Did he?" Spines asked, desperately hoping he was wrong. But he knew the answer to his question before it left his lips. Sariel stared back at him and nodded dumbly.

But how? He had designed the machine with

skills known only in the Woodbine. He knew the boy was special, that he was destined to do great things, but he hadn't counted on *this*.

There was barely time to react to the noise in the back of the room. Spines was about to turn when he felt huge, meaty hands grab the back of his coat and hoist him into the air.

"WHERE IS HE?" Whiplash Scruggs demanded, his jowls quivering with rage. Spines glanced past him and saw fifty Groundlings pour into the room. The twisted creatures all held flaming Oroboruses at the ready.

"He's gone," Spines gasped. His eyes inadvertently glanced at the smoking machine. Scruggs noticed. He stared at the machine for a long moment before comprehending.

"So, you've sent him there," he said in a low, dangerous voice. Spines felt the grip on his coat collar tighten. The fabric on the back of his jacket was pulled tightly against his swollen skin, making him moan in pain.

Scruggs didn't seem to notice. His face was beet red and his eyes flashed dangerously. The fact that he'd narrowly missed capturing Edward stung deeply, and it was all he could do to keep from reaching out and killing Melchior on the spot.

He moved his face inches in front of Melchior's own. When he spoke, his voice was a soft, dangerous whisper.

"My hounds can track him twice as well in the Woodbine, Melchior. You think you've won?" he chuckled darkly. "Not yet, old friend. The boy will soon be ours." He grinned, showing rows of pointed, white teeth. "I'm going to have you sent directly to the Jackal himself. He's been wanting to make an example of you, to show the others what happens when you break a contract."

He tossed Mr. Spines roughly to the ground. Then he stood, towering above them with his meaty fists on his hips.

"As for your two idiot servants," he glanced at Sariel and Artemis with a look of disgust. "Lilith and Asmoday would love a chance to visit with them a while. Maybe even sit down and have a meal together. Wouldn't that be nice?"

Artemis whimpered with fright, eliciting a chorus of grating laughter from the throng of Groundlings.

Turning to his Groundling officer, Scruggs barked, "Lieutenant, arrange for departure to the Woodbine immediately. I want that boy in our possession within the hour."

✦ Chapter Twenty-Two ✦

STORM

Edward pressed the sequence of buttons and switches that turned on Mr. Spines's machine. He ignored Sariel's shouts of protest as he flipped the final switch, marked ENGAGE.

Suddenly, a loud humming noise filled the air. Edward took a couple of steps backward, staring at the spinning dials. He heard the sudden whine of hidden engines reverberating all around him.

Sariel screamed.

There was a shower of sparks and a crackle of ozone. The room suddenly faded away and Edward heard the panicked shouts of Sariel and Artemis. And then, the next thing he knew, he was standing in total darkness in the middle of a thunderstorm.

Where am I? Icy drops quickly permeated his

sweater and plastered his hair to his forehead. He shivered and tried to make sense of where he was. He could hardly see anything at all.

Is this the place you go when you die? Edward wondered. It certainly wasn't like anything he'd ever expected. He strained to see through the curtains of rain and darkness.

A bright flash of lightning suddenly illuminated his surroundings. In that split second he observed that he stood on a muddy plateau with a few scraggly oaks surrounding it.

It was a quick glimpse, but he knew with overwhelming certainty that he was indeed somewhere *else*. Somewhere that was nowhere near Bunker Hill, Los Angeles, Oregon, or even the United States.

He had the sudden feeling of déjà vu, as if something deep inside him recognized the place even though he'd never been there before. And in a strange way, it seemed that his new surroundings felt more real than any of the places he'd ever lived. It was hard to explain, but it was like the mud was *muddier* and the rain felt *wetter*. It was as though everything his senses had perceived before that moment was an imperfect reflection of where he now found himself.

He took a few cautious steps forward, hoping that another flash of lightning would occur so he could see the edge of the plateau. He couldn't tell if he was on top of a mountain or just a few feet off the ground. He felt his way carefully through the darkness with his arms extended, hoping that he wouldn't trip.

BOOM! A peal of thunder crackled through the air. Then, in a sudden, panic-filled moment, Edward felt the ground beneath his feet start to crumble.

With a surge of fear he realized that he'd reached the edge of the plateau much sooner than he'd anticipated! He toppled backward as the damp earth gave way beneath his feet. In a rush of water, dirt, and stone, he cascaded down the sides of what he realized now was a very high mountain. What he hadn't known was that the plateau he'd been standing on was actually the very top of a needle-like spire and could be seen from miles away. The heavy rain had created a river that flowed down its steep sides and

Edward was tossed and carried helplessly forward like a leaf in a stream.

He had no time to think. His heart pounded with fear as he grabbed desperately for anything that might slow his fall. But nothing was anchored in the raging flow of debris.

He choked on the mud and silt that filled his mouth and nostrils. His body skidded and twisted down the mountain with tremendous speed. He sputtered and gasped for air as he fell, terrified at what would happen when he hit bottom. It seemed like he'd been falling for hours when suddenly he had the sickening sensation of weightlessness. Air rushed around him as Edward shot over the edge of the muddy waterfall.

SPLASH! He submerged beneath the surface of a raging river. The icy water engulfed him and he felt himself being dragged down to the dark and murky depths. Panic gripped him as he flailed beneath the water. He didn't know how to swim! As he felt the air slip from his lungs, a single thought resounded in his terrified brain:

What happens if you die in the Afterlife?

Chapter Twenty-Three

CATCH OF THE DAY

At the banks of the river, a faun was fishing. He didn't mind the rain that drenched his tweed hat and formed large puddles around his cloven hooves. He whistled softly to himself, thinking how much the weather reminded him of a place where he'd lived long ago.

But for Jack the faun, England was nothing but a distant memory now.

He reached into his tackle box and pulled out an unusual lure. He smiled as he removed the glowing, clockwork device.

"This should definitely do the trick," he said quietly, winding his fishing line around the lure.

With an expert flick of his wrist, Jack sent the wriggling lure sailing through the air, where it splashed into the rushing water. Jack rotated the reel on his fishing pole a few times, allowing the mechanical lure to drift in the current and settle near the bottom.

"Now," he muttered. "Let's see if we can't get some nice fish for supper."

It wasn't but a few seconds later when he felt a sudden, heavy pull on the end of his line. With a whoop of excitement, the faun cranked the reel on his pole. Whatever he had caught was huge! It was bigger than anything he'd ever caught in the river before. *A monster!* he thought happily.

He grunted as he strained to pull his catch to shore. As it drew closer, Jack let out a cry of amazement. It wasn't a fish at all.

It was a person!

"Tollers!" he shouted. "Come quickly!"

High up on the bank was a cozy inn surrounded by towering pine trees. A green door banged open and a very short man with large, furry feet emerged, huffing and puffing as he ran down the muddy slope to where Jack was standing.

"What is it?" he asked.

"I seem to have caught . . . someone," Jack cried, rushing down to the edge of the water.

"Help me get him to shore."

It required a lot of effort for the small creatures to bring the tall, waterlogged boy to the bank. By the time they had him propped between them on the shore, the heavy rain had stopped. As a large, yellow moon crept out from behind a cloud, they got their first look at the big, ebony wings that clung to Edward's wet shoulders.

"By the mane," Jack muttered. "He looks like a Guardian!"

They turned the unconscious boy on his stomach and Tollers set to work. He pushed his gnarled little hands deep into boy's back, trying to expel the river water that had filled his lungs. After a few tense moments, Edward suddenly coughed, spewing water onto the muddy ground beside him. He rolled onto his side and drew deep, shuddering breaths of the cool air.

"Let's get him inside," Jack said.

Edward was dimly aware of a pair of beings placing his arms around their shoulders as they half-carried, half-dragged him to the cozy inn by the riverbank.

A concerned murmur rose from the

patrons as Jack and Tollers entered the warmly lit common room, carrying a groggy Edward between them.

"Make way!" Jack bellowed, scattering the guests before him as he and Tollers dragged Edward to the blazing hearth. After propping him up next to the fire, he called, "Bridgette! Fetch some Bippleberry brandy!"

A pretty girl with curly red hair appeared moments later, carrying a tray with a rather dusty bottle and a small glass. As she delivered it to Jack, she gazed down at Edward, who had his eyes closed and was slumped against the side of the fireplace. His face was very pale.

"Is he going to be all right, Uncle?" she asked worriedly.

Jack uncorked the bottle and poured a small amount of purple liquid into the glass. "I believe so," he said as he raised the liquid to Edward's lips.

The hot liquid immediately sent Edward into a coughing fit, but soon he felt warmth spread throughout his body. Feeling revived, he opened his eyes and got his first clear look at his rescuers.

Seeing the friendly, concerned face of a faun staring at him was certainly a surprise. He stared back at him with his mouth hanging open in astonishment.

"I think he's going to be fine," Jack said with a relieved smile.

"Wh-where am I?" Edward asked weakly.

"You're in the Dancing Faun, the best pub south of the Seven Bridges Road," Jack said cheerfully. He studied Edward curiously. "You're lucky I was fishing. Why on Earth did you decide to enter by the river? You should have come in by the main entrance. Not really the best weather for a swim, I should think."

Edward stared back at him, confused. He had no idea what he was talking about.

The faun reached inside the soggy pocket of his tweed coat and removed a small clay pipe. He lit it and gazed at Edward's massive black wings. "How strange," he mumbled.

"Wh-what?" Edward asked.

"That you should choose to appear as a Guardian. When most mortals arrive in the Woodbine they resemble other things."

So, I really am in the Woodbine, Edward thought excitedly. *Mr. Spines's machine worked! I'm actually in the Afterlife!* He could hardly believe it.

"I d-don't understand. Wh-what do you mean I 'chose' to resemble a Guardian?" he asked.

Jack smiled and said, "When a mortal arrives in the Woodbine, he takes on the appearance of his 'inner' person. The way a person looked on Earth doesn't always match the appearance that fits him best. Up here, a person looks like what he's always *wanted* to be."

"Hence my appearance." He indicated himself with a sweeping gesture. "And theirs, too." Jack pointed to the other patrons of the cozy inn. Edward gaped at the metal unicorns with Swiss-army-knife horns that sat in one corner drinking beer. They seemed to be in an argument about something.

Suddenly, the largest one slammed his silver hoof on the table and shouted, "That wasn't the way it was at all! The third one was coming at me at four o'clock. I fired my guns six times and shot off his left rudder. I know what I saw!"

Edward glanced past them to the biggest praying mantis he had ever seen. The gigantic, pale green insect was at least six feet tall and wore silken, Chinese robes. It met Edward's stare and craned its long neck forward to get a better look at him.

Edward glanced away self-consciously. At a nearby table was a group of little men with large furry feet. They smoked their pipes, commenting quietly on Edward's unexpected arrival. And beside them was a medium-sized giant. Edward noticed that he was sleeping with his big head resting on a platter of fish and chips.

It was all too strange to believe.

The faun interrupted his thoughts, pointing at Edward's wings with the stem of his pipe. "You look like a Guardian, which is a very unusual choice," he said, grinning. "Very creative. I congratulate you on your innovation."

"Oh, but I-I didn't ch-choose this. Muh-my wings just grew y-yesterday, back on Earth. I'm actually here t-to find someone," Edward said, fighting to keep the stutter out of his voice. "I c-came here so that I could find my mother," he blurted eagerly.

The entire pub fell silent. Now it was the faun's turn to look astonished. He leaned back on the wooden bench with his hands on his knees, staring at Edward as if he'd just said something impossible. Then after a moment, he helped Edward to his feet, saying in a too-loud voice, "Yes, yes, what you need is a good night's sleep." He looked at the other patrons in the inn and winked. "Fell in the river, you know. Quite disoriented."

This explanation seemed to satisfy the others in the pub and the clatter of cutlery and murmured conversation soon recommenced. Jack noticed Edward's confused expression and whispered, "We'll talk upstairs."

Edward had no idea why what he'd said provoked such a reaction, but he followed the faun up a set of sturdy oak stairs to a hallway filled with doors. Jack motioned for Bridgette and Tollers to follow.

Inside of one of the cozy rooms, Edward sat down on the edge of a soft bed covered with patchwork quilts. A fire was crackling in the fireplace and there was a basket of sweet bread and fruit displayed on a small table. Tollers and Bridgette slipped through the doorway as Jack shut and locked the door behind them. Then the faun strode over to a stuffed chair beside Edward and sat down.

"Now then," Jack said quietly. "Some proper introductions are in order." He indicated the little man with the large, furry feet. "This is Tollers: He was the one who helped rescue you."

Edward nodded and the little man smiled back. The faun continued, "I'm Jack, and this is my niece, Bridgette."

Edward glanced up at the pretty girl. He'd always felt uncomfortable around girls his own age. At the Foundry, the girls made him feel self-conscious because of his gangly height and speech impediment. Now that he had wings, he probably looked even more ridiculous. He edged his big wings behind his back, trying to hide them from view. Feeling afraid that he might stutter if he tried too elaborate an introduction, he simply muttered, "I'm Edward," and glanced downward, turning bright crimson.

Jack smiled and placed his pipe back in his pocket. Then, leaning forward, he said, "Now, Edward, if you don't mind, I think we'd all like to know a little bit more about you. Please tell your story from the beginning and leave nothing out."

Edward felt the eyes of everyone in the room staring at him as the faun added, "Now then, I believe you said that you sprouted wings only yesterday?"

Edward nodded, wishing that he didn't have to speak. But, with three expectant faces turned toward him, it seemed that he had no choice but to do as Jack asked.

He sighed. And then, hoping his stutter wouldn't embarrass him too much, he began to tell them all about the series of events that had led him to the Woodbine.

✦ Chapter Twenty-Four ✦

THE BLUE LADY

Edward told them about his mother's death, his life at the Foundry, his meeting Mr. Spines, and escaping Whiplash Scruggs. There were many gasps of astonishment as he mentioned the run-in with Henry and Lilith. And by the time he finished his story, several hours had passed.

Jack and Tollers shared a look as Edward wrapped up his tale. Turning back to Edward, the faun said, "Please excuse Tollers and me for a few moments. I'm afraid your tale has given us some rather, ah, important matters to discuss."

Then Jack and Tollers walked over to the corner of the room and began talking rapidly in low, secretive voices.

Bridgette noticed and rolled her eyes. Grinning, she turned back to Edward and said, "My uncle and Tollers are constantly doing research on the Guardians and the Jackal. When they were mortals on Earth they were professors. Your story's really got them excited. It's really rare for a mortal, especially one with such beautiful wings, to come to the Woodbine."

Then she smiled at him in such a warm and dazzling way that Edward forgot about how silly he thought his wings looked.

Bridgette continued, saying, "I think you were very brave doing what you did, facing those Groundlings. If I'd run into Asmoday and Lilith, I think I probably would have fainted."

Edward chuckled. "I really had no idea what I was doing. I was able to fight them somehow. It happened without my even trying." He didn't realize it, but there was something so comforting about the way Bridgette was talking to him that he didn't stutter once.

Jack and Tollers's urgent discussion continued, escalating into an argument. Bridgette didn't seem bothered, so Edward continued the conversation with her, saying, "So what were some of the other people downstairs? Back when they were on Earth, I mean."

Bridgette grinned hugely. "You'll never guess. The unicorns were soldiers in the Great War. They fought with the Allies in France." She lowered her voice to a whisper. "Some of them aren't very nice. Uncle Jack thinks that one or two of them might be agents of the Jackal sent to spy on the Inn, but I really don't think so." She glanced over at her uncle, who was so absorbed in his conversation he hadn't heard.

She counted off each of the remaining patrons on her fingers. "The mantis was a Chinese philosopher and she's over a thousand years old. She's really nice and loves to play dominoes. The little men with the furry feet were students of Tollers when he was a professor. And as for the giant . . ." Her eyes twinkled as she grinned down at Edward. "You'll never guess what he used to be."

"What was he?" Edward asked, feeling curious about the hulking man he'd seen snoring in the corner.

"He was a librarian! He said he was really short and skinny and wore glasses!" She laughed and the sound was so wonderfully pretty and contagious that Edward found himself laughing, too.

Jack and Tollers finally finished their discussion and turned back to Edward, their faces alight with excitement.

"Edward, Tollers and I think your arrival is very auspicious, *very* auspicious indeed! We have a lot of research to do back at my house. Once we consult my books, we'll be able to tell you more about what we know. My wife Joyce loves company, and I'm sure she would love for you to stay with us."

Edward didn't know what to say at first. Everything had happened so quickly that he'd never even considered where he would stay once he'd arrived in the Woodbine. All he'd been thinking about at the time was getting to his mother. But there was something so wonderful about the new people he'd met. There was something about them that radiated trust, and that was something Edward hadn't felt for a long time.

He glanced at Bridgette and she echoed her uncle's comment, saying, "It really would be great if you'd stay with us. You'll love it there. We have a forest near the house and we can go exploring . . ." Her face brightened as if remembering something. "Oh, and the Woodhaven Festival starts tomorrow afternoon! You have to stay! The festival is so amazing!"

There was no way he could resist. Seeing a girl like Bridgette smiling at him, actually *wanting* to spend time with him, had never happened before. He felt a surge of happiness at the thought of having friends and a warm place to stay. Immensely grateful, Edward smiled and said, "Thank you. I-I'd love to."

Then he turned to Jack and asked, "But d-do you know anything about my mother? Mr. Spines said she n-needed my help and is imprisoned in the Jackal's fortress. H-her name was Sarah Jane Macleod."

For the second time that night, Jack looked completely stunned. Recovering himself, he asked, "Your mother is the Blue Lady?"

Seeing his confused expression, Jack quickly moved to a small bookshelf next to the bed where Edward was sitting and removed a large leather volume. He flipped through several pages and stopped at a picture. Then he handed the book to Edward.

Edward stared down at the beautifully colored illustration. A woman dressed in flowing blue robes was riding a winged horse and carrying an elegant spear. As his eyes traveled up the picture to the woman's face his heart stopped. The familiar, gentle brown eyes of his mother stared back at him.

He was too overcome to speak.

The faun offered him a kind smile and said, "Edward, your mother is a great hero in the Woodbine. Everyone knows her. She has fought the Jackal's forces with as much strength and dedication as a Guardian."

Edward wiped his burning eyes with the back of his hand, trying to grasp what the faun was saying. His mother? A warrior?

"There m-must be a mistake," he said softly. "Are you s-sure you mean *my* mother?"

Jack put his hand on Edward's shoulder and said, "Not all people go to the Higher Places when they die. Those that reside in the Woodbine have unfinished business still on Earth."

He smiled kindly. "Your mother must have loved you very much. She often spoke of the son from whom she believed she had been taken too soon."

The faun paused for a moment. Then he said, "There have always been rumors that the Jackal had a secret way out of the Woodbine hidden in the depths of his fortress. Your mother told the Guardians that she didn't care how impossible it was, she was going to find a way back to Earth to be with her son. She slew over two hundred of the enemy's soldiers before they finally captured and imprisoned her."

Edward's eyes were so filled with tears that he had to look away from the picture in the book. All this time, while he was at the Foundry feeling alone and forgotten, his mother was watching over him, fighting for a chance to see him again.

The thought filled him with a renewed sense of belonging, something he thought he'd lost forever. Life wasn't meaningless. It didn't end on Earth. There were some things that went on forever.

He wiped his eyes on the sleeve of his sweater.

"But she's still here?" he asked.

"Yes, she is. But getting to her might be impossible . . ." Jack began.

"I'll find her," he said firmly.

Edward carefully placed the book with his mother's picture next to the pillow on the bed. Then he stood up with his big, ebony wings flaring out on either side of him.

He looked every inch a Guardian. The others watched as he flexed his back muscles, causing his wings to make two powerful flaps. It was the first time he'd ever tried to use them for what they were intended for. And as they pushed through the air, Edward could feel his feathers quiver, itching to soar on gentle breezes. He knew with certainty that these wings would carry him to his mother's prison. He wouldn't look at them as a deformity or be embarrassed by them any longer.

"I'll be right back," he said.

The others watched as Edward walked to the door at the other end of the small room. The tall boy stepped outside onto the balcony with his wings drifting behind him like a long, feathered cape.

The storm had passed. Edward felt a cool wind ruffle through his feathers and he breathed in the damp, earthy air.

He gazed at the star-filled heavens and smiled.

It was an excellent night to fly.

Appendix

GLOSSARY OF TERMS

Achiyon:

Another name for the Jackal. Literally "Destroyer" in Guardian tongue. *See also* Belial.

Agareas:

A Groundling and the Jackal's chief emissary. Often seen as an old man riding a crocodile.

Al:

Also known as Al the Boatman. Al's a ferryman in the Woodbine who transports passengers across the dangerous, memory-erasing waters of the river Lithye. He is also one of the few mortals who asked for permanent residence in the Woodbine. In addition to serving as ferryman, Al is known to be a fisherman of great skill. "The Catch of the Scarlet Wingfish" was a song composed in his honor by popular musician and Guardian, Zapeth Silversong. It's said that the fish took over two weeks to capture due to its ability to swim both underwater and in the air.

Angel's Flight:

A funicular train in Los Angeles that leads to the top of a wealthy neighborhood called Bunker Hill. *See also* Bunker Hill.

Artemis:

An apprentice to Melchior, Chief Musician of the Seven Worlds. Artemis fell with Melchior and Sariel in W.R.[1] 1255. Due to the Corruption, Artemis resembles a flying green toad. Artemis's Guardian parents were Shemial and Selenia. Both were killed in a skirmish with the Groundlings. *See also* Sariel *and* Melchior.

1 Woodbine Reckoning Calendar

Asmoday:

Also known as Henry Asmoday. Asmoday is a high-ranking Groundling in the Jackal's army. Most scholars believe Asmoday fell almost three hundred years after the Jackal, (W.R. 362). Asmoday is the royal escort for Lilith, the Jackal's Queen. Prior to his fall, Asmoday was a lieutenant under Commander Mik'ael. While serving as a Guardian he was decorated twice for bravery. He was a recipient of the Feathered Cross, 2nd Class, for bravery during the Zephyr Skirmish and was decorated for his strategic victory in the Battle of Arioch. He's considered by most Guardians to be an extremely cunning adversary and is an expert at hiding his tracks.

B

Beaudry, Prudent:

Benefactor of Mr. Spines. Mr. Beaudry's descendants allow Spines the use of his home when in Los Angeles.

Belial:

The Jackal's earliest recorded name. In

Guardian tongue, *Belial* means "Bridge Breaker." He was one of the first Guardians to fall from the Woodbine. His reasons for falling are known only to himself, but many speculate that it was because he couldn't obtain a more prestigious rank in the Higher Places. *See also* Jackal.

Blue Snail:
Also called "Buruch." Gigantic creature with the body of a snail and the head of an elderly human. Blue Snails are the repositories of lore for Cornelius, a famous Guardian ringmaker in the Woodbine. In times of great need, the snails can transform into fearsome fighters. *See also* Cornelius.

Bradbury Building:
The Jackal's headquarters on Earth and place of transport for his forces to the Woodbine. Considered by many to be the most evil place in Los Angeles.

Bridge Builder, the:

The prophetic son of a Guardian and a mortal that will rebuild the bridges between the worlds that the Jackal destroyed. *See also* Seven Bridges.

Bridges:

See Seven Bridges.

Bridgette:

Adopted niece of Jack the faun, an expert in Woodbine lore.

Brimstone Mines:

Another name for the Charon Fields, the Jackal's special place of punishment reserved for his disobedient troops. There are some Groundlings that have been sentenced there for more than three thousand years.

Bunker Hill:

Not to be confused with the famous Bunker Hill in Massachusetts, it is the name for a wealthy section of town in 1920s Los Angeles.

C

Cornelius:

Keeper of the Blue Snails in the Woodbine. An ancient Guardian of indeterminate age.

Corruption, the:

A crippling disease that affects fallen Guardians that haven't joined the Jackal's forces.

D

Dancing Faun, the:

An inn near the spot where mortals' souls arrive when transported to the Woodbine. It is also a popular destination for Jack and Tollers. It's a cozy place where evenings of discussion, good food, and drink are in abundance. The first reference to the inn appears in a letter from the Guardian Beshumiel in a letter dated W.R. 107. It states: ". . . there's no greater place to meet mortals than the Faun. In fact, I met a wonderful two-headed griffin that used to be a seamstress in Liverpool, England, yesterday and learned more about needles and thread than I ever needed to know."

Fall, the:

The great rebellion of the Jackal and his forces. "Falling" is also the term used to refer to the point when a Guardian chooses to leave the Woodbine and join the enemy forces.

Foundry, the:

A trade school that trains its students for practical careers. Usually this training encompasses areas of study that are considered distasteful by most job seekers, giving the graduates an excellent chance of employment.

Grigori:

See Watchers *and* Melchior.

Groundling:

A nickname for fallen Guardians. Reserved especially for those who serve the Jackal.

Grudgel, John:

Edward's enemy at the Foundry. Known by the nickname "Grudge." After escaping from the Foundry, John wandered the streets of

Portland for several weeks, trying to find a way home to his parents in Astoria. After seeking transportation in a disreputable tavern, John Grudgel was pressed into service aboard a merchant vessel. Twenty years later a record was found of a prominent dentist named John Grudgel in the Fiji Islands. A diary entry from Grudgel mentioned his love for dentistry happening at a young age after the misfortune of biting down on a ball bearing and cracking two molars.

Guardian:

Protectors assigned to watch over mortals and engage the Jackal's forces in combat.

H

Henry Asmoday:

See Asmoday.

***Histalek*:**

A Guardian word of power, translated as "begone." The secret words, or "The Ten," are typically reserved for high commanders in the Guardian Army.

I

Ignatius, Mr.:

A Groundling stationed at the Foundry to spy on Edward.

J

Jack the Faun:

A mortal that now resides in the Woodbine. On Earth, he was a professor of medieval literature. Jack is highly respected for his exhaustive research on Guardian lore.

Jackal, the:

The ancient enemy of the Guardians. Other names for the Jackal include Belial and Achiyon. Both Groundlings and Guardians commonly use the "Jackal" nickname due to his high-pitched, barking laugh. When he fell, most of his physical body was torn apart by the bridges he destroyed. He is now rumored to be more machine than Guardian.

Joyce:

Jack the faun's wife. As a mortal, Joyce was a prolific poet and well known for her exceptional marksmanship. In the Woodbine she often helps young Guardians learn to use their rings as projectile weapons.

L

Lair, Jackal's:
The term used to refer to the Jackal's Woodbine fortress. Not to be confused with the Bradbury Building in Los Angeles, where the Jackal's terrestrial headquarters are located.

Lilith:
The Jackal's Queen. Lilith is known for her ruthless treatment of mortals.

M

Machine, the:
An invention designed by Mr. Spines to transport himself to the Woodbine. There has been much speculation about the method of construction for this ingenious device. In the Woodbine, Mr. Spines (Melchior) is known to be an excellent designer and craftsman.

Macleod, Edward:
The son of a mortal and a Guardian with an

exceptional talent for building elaborate card houses.

Macleod, Sarah Jane:

Edward's mother, known as the "Blue Lady" in the Woodbine. Sarah Macleod was the only mortal in history to marry a fallen Guardian.

Melchior:

Mr. Spines's Guardian name.

Mines, the:

See Brimstone Mines.

Moloc:

Whiplash Scruggs's Groundling name.

Mulciber:

One of Whiplash Scruggs's two dogs. The other is Olivier. Both dogs are prized for their tracking abilities and poisonous bites.

N

***Nsh*:**

Guardian Tongue for "test." Often used by

Guardians to test a ring to make sure that it works properly. It is also used to ignite the weapon's fire.

O

Olivier:
One of Whiplash Scruggs's dogs.

Oroborus:
An imitation of a Guardian's Ring created by the Jackal. While most Guardian Rings are unadorned, the Oroborus is often molded into the form of a serpent biting its own tail. Many Woodbine scholars have debated as to whether or not the Oroborus is as effective as a Guardian Ring, but the results are inconclusive.

P

Polanski, Miss:
A Groundling stationed at the Foundry to spy on Edward.

Q

Qados:
Guardian Tongue for "light."

Ring:
The circular weapon of power used by Guardians. The Guardian Ring functions both as a dimensional portal device and as a weapon.

Sariel:
Melchior's apprentice. Sariel fell with Melchior in the year W.R. 1255. As a young Guardian, Sariel was known for her natural gift with musical instruments and was being groomed to take over Melchior's position as Chief Musician. Due to the Corruption, Sariel's form was changed after her fall from a Guardian of exceptional beauty to an ermine. *See also* Artemis.

Scruggs, Whiplash:
A nickname for Moloc, a duke in the Jackal's army. Known especially for his terrible whip and boundless cruelty.

***Se'ol*:**

"Place of the Dead." Another name for the Jackal's Lair.

Seven Bridges, the:

The bridges that the Jackal destroyed when he fell from the Higher Places. Each one of the worlds he passed by on his way down has a name and purpose. The Woodbine is counted as the first of the seven because of its proximity to Earth. It was designed as a brief stopping point for mortal souls to complete any unfinished business they left behind on Earth. Usually this takes the form of helping a Guardian care for a loved one during a time of grief.

The second world, Lelakek, is the world of feasting. It's a happy place where many mortals enjoy the company of friends and family that have passed on.

The third world is called Jubal and is a place for meditation and rest.

Little is known about the fourth world, Baradil, which is cloaked in heavy clouds. Some believe that it is a place where souls discover a new and secret purpose for their lives in the Higher Places.

The fifth world, Akamai, contains a vast music library. It's a place where souls learn how to compose Songs of Power. Out of all the worlds, Akamai is the one that the Jackal fears most. He believes there are melodies contained in the library that could bring about his ultimate destruction.

The sixth world, Zeshar, was designed without rails on the narrow bridge that leads up to it. This is because one of the tasks presented to the mortal souls on Akamai is to use their research to come up with a Song that will help them traverse the bridge. One of the favorite pastimes of those who have decided to reside at Akamai is to listen to the different melodies people have composed that allow them to travel up to the next world.

The seventh world, Iona, is the closest to the Higher Places. This mysterious world had its bridge stolen by the Jackal in W.R. 60. Many believe that it was this first act of defiance that gave him the idea to destroy the other bridges when he fell. It is interesting to note that during his fall he missed the sixth bridge on his way down, and was only able to destroy the five below it. Rumors of a replacement bridge for the seventh exist, one that is invisible to the Jackal and the Groundlings. It is said that only those whose hearts are pure can see the new bridge which was put in its place.

***Sisma*:**
Guardian tongue for "open."

Song of Power:
Used by Guardians for magical purposes. Songs of Power are designated for different purposes and require extensive training to use.

Spines, Mr.:
See Melchior.

T

Tollers:

A mortal who now resides in the Woodbine, Tollers was a professor of Anglo-Saxon literature at Oxford University while on Earth. Colleague of Jack the faun and fellow researcher of Guardian lore.

W

Warburton, Dr.:

Principal of the Foundry.

Woodbine, the:

The first of the Seven Worlds and the closest to Earth. It is the place originally designed for mortals with unfinished business to attend to on Earth. It was meant to be a place of temporary lodging, but due to the Jackal's fall and subsequent destruction of the Seven Bridges, many of the mortals have been unable to traverse to the upper worlds. *See also* Seven Bridges.

Z

***Zeh Lo Meshane*:**

Guardian Tongue for "of no consequence." A Lyric of Power used to hide from view someone who wishes to remain unnoticed.

Coming Soon:

THE MYSTERIOUS MR. SPINES

FLIGHT

ESCAPE!

Through an opened window, Edward could hear the faint barks of Whiplash Scruggs's hounds in the distance. He was terrified!

"I had nothing to do with"—gasp—"Scruggs tracking me here," Mr. Spines wheezed. His face looked haggard and pale. "The Jackal has spies posted everywhere, keeping watch on every new arrival in the Woodbine. I . . ."—gasp—"I did my best to cover my tracks, but, as you can plainly see . . ." Mr. Spines indicated to his own withered and crumpled form. "The Corruption has made it difficult for me to even move. If I don't have some medical attention soon I probably won't survive much longer."

Edward noticed that Spines seemed much smaller and uglier than when he'd first met him on the train the previous day. In fact, there were other subtle changes he hadn't noticed before. The creature had more spines growing out from beneath his stovepipe hat than ever and his jacket was riddled with holes where new spikes were starting to poke through. He was starting to look more like a monster than a man.

Mr. Spines coughed and continued. "Anyway"—wheeze—"Whiplash Scruggs doesn't care about any of you. All he wants is the boy." Melchior indicated to Edward with a sharp nod.

"W-well, h-he can't have me!" Edward shot back. He was starting to panic.

"Of course he can't," Spines said, shooting Edward a withering look. "Trust me, boy, with whatever I have left, I will fight to keep you safe from him. But we must hurry if we're to escape his notice." He turned his bloodshot eyes on Jack. "Is there"—cough—"a back door?" Melchior ran his tongue across his yellowed teeth.

Jack nodded. "Yes, Joyce had me install a passage for just such an emergency. I'll take you to it."

"You're going to help him?" Tabitha, an apprentice Guardian, asked, looking incredulous.

Jack nodded at the young Guardian. "I believe that Melchior is telling the truth. I'll do all I can to help. If he says he's against the Jackal then that's good enough for me."

There was a brief silence where Edward could hear the barking of Whiplash Scruggs's hounds growing closer. Finally Jemial, a senior Guardian who had come to help, spoke, turning to Jack.

"Is the house protected?" he asked.

"We had a couple of Guardians do a Shield Song several years back, but it probably needs to be sung again," Jack said.

"I'll try singing a Song of Warding. Hopefully it will help reinforce the shield on the cottage and hold Scruggs off for a while." The big Guardian turned to Tabitha and said, "I want you to go with them to help the boy find his mother. I also want you to keep an eye on Melchior. Report any questionable behavior to me immediately."

Tabitha looked aghast. "But they said she was captured by the Jackal. No Guardians can penetrate his lair . . ." she began, but was cut off by a curt remark from her master.

"I gave you an order! You're to protect the boy. If he really is the Bridge Builder, then I'm sure he'll surprise us all with his abilities. Go!" Jemial ordered.

Boooom! Just then, a sound like thunder rattled the interior of the cottage. Edward stared around wildly. *What was that?*

"Scruggs is attacking the shield on the cottage. Quick, follow me," Jack said, motioning to Edward, Melchior, and Tabitha.

Jemial withdrew a small flute from his pocket and began to play the Song of Warding. Bridgette pulled Jack aside.

"I'm going with them, Uncle," Bridgette said.

"No, it's too dangerous, Bridgette. Moloc is one of the most feared Groundlings in the Jackal's army. You could get seriously hurt!" Jack answered.

Bridgette looked resolute. "I'm sorry. I know you're trying to protect me, but I *need* to go." She glanced at Edward and then quickly turned back to her uncle. "Remember what we talked about? I believe that *this* is the reason I'm here, the reason I didn't go immediately to the

Higher Places like my sister."

After a long moment, Jack nodded. "So be it. Come then, all of you."

The faun trotted quickly out of the living room and down a narrow hallway. Edward followed with the others.

Boooom! The sound came again, this time from the opposite side of the house. Edward glanced outside a nearby window and saw curling wisps of yellow smoke rising from the grassy lawn.

Edward silently prayed that somehow Jemial's song would still work.

Just buy us a few minutes more so that we can escape!

Then the booming sound came again. And this time, to everyone's horror, the sound was accompanied by a loud *crack*!

Edward immediately knew what it meant.

Scruggs had broken through!

Jack rushed to a large wardrobe in the corner of his study and opened the doors to reveal a hidden passage.

"Quick, through here!" the faun commanded. "Follow this passage all the way to the end. It leads to a dock where a boatman will be waiting for you. He's a friend. I'll send word to you if I'm able. Good-bye and good luck!"

Then the faun pushed the wardrobe doors closed and the passageway was suddenly plunged into total darkness.

Edward heard a sharp, scratching noise. Then a flickering flame suddenly illuminated Mr. Spines's ugly face. The match he held was encased in a tiny, silver box covered with gears.

"Follow me!" he growled and hobbled down the damp passageway. Edward and the others followed the tiny, flickering light as it bobbed off into the distance.

Debris rained down, and several muffled explosions echoed above them. The cloying darkness of the tunnel seemed to go on forever. Then, after what seemed like an eternity, they finally reached the end. Spines shoved hard against a wooden door that was covered with spiderwebs and they tumbled forward, out of the tunnel and onto a grassy riverbank.

Edward glanced back in the direction they'd come from. Underneath the cloudy sky, Jack's cottage was glowing with an ominous shade of red. Seconds later, he realized why. The faun's house was on fire!

Edward turned away and hurried to catch up with the others. It was too much to think about.

"The docks are over there," Mr. Spines said. "Hurry."

As they struggled down the banks, the sound of baying hounds filled the air, followed by a flurry of deep-throated barks.

Spines stared in the direction of the cottage and let out a long, low hiss.

"He knows we're gone. Hurry!" And in spite of his severely weakened condition, the stunted creature shot off toward the dock.

"I'm coming!" a voice floated across the river toward them. Edward could make out a figure clad in heavy boots and a leather jerkin standing on a large boat that reminded Edward a little bit of a sturdy gondola. A stocky man was holding a long pole, and pushing the boat toward them as quickly as he could.

An eerie howl split the air, much closer than before. The skin on the back of Edward's neck prickled. Whiplash Scruggs and his Groundlings were not far behind!

"Hurry!" Tabitha shouted, her wings fluttering in agitation.

"Is there trouble?" the boatman shouted back as he poled the boat into position.

"We're being pursued by a Groundling," Mr. Spines growled.

The stocky man nodded quickly. "Hop aboard then, but be careful not to touch the water. You're on the banks of the Lethye. Can't afford to have anyone lose their marbles."

Edward had no idea what the boatman meant, but he was careful to stay dry as he climbed in. Edward glanced behind him and immediately wished he hadn't. Whiplash Scruggs was almost to the river.

"Go! Go! GO!" Edward shouted. "He's here!"

WHOOOSH! Something hot whistled past Edward's head, narrowly missing his ear. Edward raised his hand to his cheek, feeling a slight burning sensation. Fortunately, the flaming object had only singed him.

"It's an Oroborus!" Tabitha shouted. Edward turned and spotted the blazing ring as it soared over a nearby thicket of pine trees. If it had flown any closer, it would have taken his head off!

Tabitha quickly undid a clasp on her blue sash and withdrew her golden ring. "Everybody stay as far down on the deck as you can! I'll guard us from the air!"

She gazed down at her ring and shouted, "*Qados!*" Instantly, the golden hoop was encircled in a flickering ring of blue flames. Then, with a mighty downward flap of her wings, Tabitha shot off into the air.

Above the pine trees in the distance, the Oroborus had completed its arc and was now returning toward the boat, streaking toward them like a flaming comet.

A great shout went up from the riverbank and Edward looked over to see the source of the commotion. It was Whiplash Scruggs at the head of his troop of low-ranking Groundlings. The only Groundlings Edward had encountered so far had looked human, except for their unnaturally pale blue eyes and sharp teeth. But that mostly human appearance was reserved for the highest-ranked soldiers in the Jackal's army, a "costume" of sorts that hid their true, corrupted bodies. This throng of gibbering creatures on the bank was exposed as what they really were.

Edward cringed. Could such things have ever been beautiful Guardians? They were disgusting creatures that looked neither animal nor human. Many were half rotten with decay, covered with leprous sores. A few others had a misshapen wing or a crumpled bunch of feathers sticking out of their twisted backs. Their ugly faces had fangs, snouts or vulturelike beaks, and every one of them had eyes of the palest blue.

Their attention was momentarily diverted from the boat where Edward, Bridgette, and Spines were hiding and was focused instead on the young Guardian. They jeered as Tabitha dove and swooped, trying to avoid the deadly weapon that seemed to track her every movement.

She's drawing it toward herself, Edward thought. *She's putting herself in the way so that it doesn't come after me.*

Even though he had no idea how the weapon worked, Edward had guessed something close to the truth. Guardian rings sought their opposite in battle, honing in on evil like a magnet. The Oroborus had been designed to seek out Guardians and was guided to the closest enemy target with deadly accuracy. Because Tabitha was nearest, the ring was after her.

Edward could only stare, mouth agape, as he watched the Guardian fly. In spite of having wings himself, he'd never seen firsthand what could be done with them. He watched her every move as she dove and swooped majestically through the air. He'd never seen such an amazing sight.

And for the first time ever, he saw the true power of a Guardian in flight.

When the Oroborus got too close, Tabitha used her own ring as a shield. Edward watched flashes of red fire collide with blue sparks as Tabitha successfully deflected each of the weapon's successive attacks with her slim, golden circle.

Edward had nearly forgotten about Whiplash Scruggs because he was so busy watching Tabitha's performance. But he was brought back to the present when he heard the fearsome commander bellow an order to his soldiers.

Up in the sky, Tabitha continued her acrobatic dance, narrowly avoiding the Oroborus. Edward could tell that she was getting tired. She wasn't making as many fancy loops and dives anymore. It seemed to take all of her strength just to deflect the relentless ring.

Then, something completely unexpected happened. All of the Groundlings gave a shout, saying the same, guttural word in unison.

"Nsh!"

A dozen circles of red flames appeared in each of the Groundlings' fists. Edward had mistakenly thought that Whiplash Scruggs had possessed the only one! With a shout the other Groundlings threw their Oroboruses into the air, hurtling them toward the sole defender that hovered above Edward's boat.

Edward's mind raced. If he didn't do something fast, Tabitha would be cut to ribbons!

Suddenly, like it had once before, an unknown word popped into his mind. It was the same word that he'd used before to repel an attack from Lilith and Asmoday, two of the Jackal's most powerful servants. He could feel a tingling sensation building inside of him as he turned his head skyward, determining an angle where the swiftly moving evil rings could be intercepted. Then, after steadying himself for the tremendous burst of energy that was sure to come, he stood up on the deck. Extending his fingers in the direction of the flaming weapons he shouted, "*Histalek!*"

There was a flash of blue light and the burning smell of ozone. Lightning arced from Edward's extended fingertips, snaking skyward to intercept the dozen hoops of red fire.

Kerraccckkk! The electric shock from Edward's fingertips impacted the evil rings with a tremendous explosion of sparks.

Broken pieces of Oroborus showered down all around him, peppering the water with little splashes. Edward swayed on his feet. It felt as if all the strength he possessed had drained from his body.

His eyes lost focus as the world spun crazily around him.

He heard a muffled shout from Bridgette as his legs folded beneath him and his long body crashed down toward the bottom of the boat, landing with a *thunk*! He didn't see his deck of cards tumble from his pocket and fall into the water as he hit the hard, wooden deck.

Everything went black.